LORD OF THE TWO LANDS

Ian Lancaster

Afraid for the succession, a young king knows he must prove himself worthy before the gods. His chance comes in a most unexpected way when a new friend becomes a deadly enemy. This is the eighth and final part of the Egypt saga.

LORD OF THE TWO LANDS

From the enormous window in his private quarters, high within the walls of the ancient royal palace, Tarka looked out across the vast desert over which he now reigned supreme. It had been a long journey, he had not been destined to rule, but once started he had found it surprisingly easy. He had never been a favourite of his father, and his elder brother had little time for him as he prepared for his own, inevitable, succession. He was not sure when the idea first came to him, probably on one of his long solitary walks in the desert that he loved, but once the idea was formed it grew until it obsessed him. Why should he not rule? Did the gods not favour the bold, those prepared to risk all for a cause they believed in? And Tarka certainly believed in himself.

His father was well guarded and he had the self-confidence of an old man surrounded by his faithful subjects. He had reigned for so long that many of his people had known no other king and could not imagine a world in which he was not their guardian and their guide. And his brother, sickeningly handsome and the model of the perfect soldier, he would step forward when the time came, to take his place on the jewelled throne. There was no place for Tarka in the carefully ordered world into which he had been born. He was just the 'spare' son that, thanks to the gods, didn't seem to be needed after all. But the gods were not always in control, and a man confident in his own destiny could surely change the future.

He had planned his course well. He needed help, of course, and so he sought out those whose own lives also seemed destined for frustration. A couple of middle-ranking priests, never likely to achieve a more exalted position, an ambitious army officer constantly overlooked for promotion, royal servants who felt that they could achieve so much more if given the opportunity. He singled them out, took them into his care, gave them his patronage, and gradually, very gradually, made them believe that they could all gain so much more, more wealth, more power, more of everything, if he was king instead. And so, when he finally revealed his plans to them, they were already his to command.

He decided that a single, bloody night of killing would not be the answer. He wanted them to beg him to be king, he did not want to seem to have seized the throne. He did not want to start his reign seeming to have offended the orderly plans laid by the gods. His father could die of old age, that could certainly be arranged, and no-one would guess the help he had given with his own hands and one of the enormous soft cushions which propped the old man up in his great bed. Then, while the people were mourning their king, he would arrange to expose his brother as unfit to take the throne. Young men would come forward to tell of the nights they had been debauched by the prince, letters would be found to suggest that he had been giving royal jewels and gold, and even royal favours, to boost his popularity, even that a murder had been concealed, of a servant girl strangled with his own hands, who had threatened to expose him. And then, before any claims could be investigated too thoroughly, Tarka would have his own military guard take control of the army, its generals clearly complicit in the corruption, as well as the senior priests who surely must have been aware and did nothing. He would have his own men, his trusted acolytes, in place to seize control just when they were needed. He would then address the nobles, expressing his horror at all that had been uncovered, and would then, reluctantly, agree to take control and be crowned as the new king. His new chief priest would ensure that the ceremonies were completed as quickly as possible and nothing would ever be heard again of his brother or the others who had been sacrificed for his success. His followers would be well rewarded, as promised, and his position secured by the loyalty of the priests and the army. The people would simply be told that a new order now ruled. As long as they were bribed with appropriate feast days and celebrations, they would be no wiser. Their lives would continue as before.

And so it had been. He had only taken time from his busy scheming to watch his brother being tortured to death in rooms deep beneath the palace, where the thick mud-brick walls absorbed his screams. Some compensation anyway for the years when his brother had ignored him. He buried his father with honour, days of feasts and ceremonies to make the people forget that so many other changes had occurred. And he appeared to his people, his people as they now were, to assure them they were in safe hands now that all of the corruption had been rooted out.

Now the world was his, and he cast his greedy eyes to the north, across the hot desert sands to another land, a land of unbelievable riches, ruled by a boy king who surely would be no match for someone who had so ruthlessly and so cleverly just become master of his own destiny. A land where all was centred on a single, mighty river, a river which ran through his own kingdom first. A land ripe for the taking.

PART 1

Kamose

It was in that first hour after the mighty sun had started its journey across the sky that I missed them the most. I always loved this time, my time. The only time in the day I could truly call my own. My most beloved wife Reja would still be sleeping, breathing softly, her long dark hair framing her beautiful face, the palace would be quiet with just the distant sounds of servants preparing the first meals of the day, and the great river was still largely empty of boats. There would be bustle and noise soon enough, as everyone else started their day, but, for the moment anyway, I felt that I had the world to myself.

It was then that I would sit on the wide terrace overlooking the river and think of family. It seemed so long ago that we had all been together. After Reja and I had been married and after the great reunion that had brought them all safely back to me, at least six summers ago. But they had lives of their own, other kingdoms to take care of, and it would have been selfish of me to ask them to stay longer. Kitane and Itaja were the first to leave, saying a tearful farewell to their beloved daughter, now my wife and queen of this great land. Itaja had to travel far to the north to be with his own ailing father, king of another great land, and to be sure that his brother had support for his own succession. Kitane felt that she had neglected her people for long enough and they had much to do to repair the ravages of the Sea People. I was able to persuade my mother and Rusa to stay for a while longer but I could see how anxious they were to return as well. Rusa had great responsibilities of his own and my mother had decided that she wanted to be with him on the island, and close to Kitane, now that

I had a wife of my own to care for me. They stayed until Rusa had given valuable guidance to my own captains about the great seas they would now be travelling more often, guidance which they accepted willingly from one who knew so much, but he would not accept my offer of a permanent place at court as my Chief of Navy. He did, however, recommend one who should be considered for that role, and my uncle Amasis was even now at sea training new captains to develop their skills. It had been a wonderful time when they were here. I had grown to love and respect Rusa as a man, as a husband for my dear mother, and, of course, as my father. This was not something for anyone else to know, not even my beloved wife knew. To everyone else, to all of my people and to all in lands around, I was the son and legitimate heir of the great king Senwasre, I was Lord of the Two Lands, and this was a position I had now held for some twelve summers.

We kept in touch, of course, and I knew that they were all well, but I missed them and looked for any excuses for them to visit or for Reja and I to visit them. It had been three summers since Reja and I had last visited the great island, for only a few short weeks, and I know my wife wanted to share with her mother the enormous sadness she felt at so recently losing yet another of our unborn children. This was the second child she had lost, not even close to the full time, and the physicians had told me it had been another boy. We had prayed to the gods to ask them what we had done that they should hurt us in this way, putting the kingdom itself in peril for want of an heir, but there had been no sign, no guidance for how we could make things right with them. But we would keep trying and it in no way diminished my love for Reja or made me consider seeking an heir with anyone else. I could have other wives, as many as I wished, but I wanted only one. She was my best friend and my dearest companion. My son and heir would be her son as well. That I vowed to the gods. But I was unsure of the message they were sending to me. I could only think that they were concerned that any son of mine would not be a true and legitimate heir to the throne of Senwasre, the man who had loved me as a father and whose lands and whose titles I took for my own upon his death. I would have to prove myself to be worthy, to earn the title of king for myself. Only then would they consider my son to be worthy as well.

On this particular morning I had an important meeting to prepare for, and so my time of peaceful reverie was short. Another was soon to leave me and I knew I would miss him as much as I missed my parents. Teti had been frail for some time now, bowed down by the enormity of his responsibilities as vizier of this great land, and I had urged him to reduce his load by training others to take more of the work from him. We had now divided up his office into a number of parts, each supervised by competent scribes and ministers, and we were watching them carefully to see who, in the end, might succeed him. Today he was to leave the capital and return to his old home in the north, the old capital city where he had lived for so long, to rejoin his wives Kashta and Nefret, and to begin a much-deserved retirement. I could call upon him if I needed his advice, of course, but I vowed that I would not disturb his peace unless it was really necessary. But first he and I would meet with my most senior army commanders, Nehsi and Huya, and we would consider the invitation I had received from the new king of the lands far beyond our southern borders. This man, Tarka, had just succeeded his father and was anxious to meet with me to discuss our trading agreements and to pledge mutual support and loyalty. We had good relations with his father, his lands provided us with many valuable and exotic goods, and there seemed no reason to think that anything had changed. A royal visit to his lands would enhance his prestige with his people and could benefit us as well. It would give my wife a much-needed break from courtly routine, and might even help her to smile again. She smiles for the people, and for all who meet her, but I know she is not smiling inside. I so much want her to smile again and to mean it. She has the most wonderful smile.

Reja

I knew he valued this time alone. He thought he had left me asleep but how could I not know that he had left my arms. The first time I was concerned for him and went to find him, but the sight as he sat on the terrace, the sun newly risen in the sky, looking with such sadness at the great river beyond, made me pause and not wish to disturb his thoughts or his memories. We had just lost the chance to be parents and I knew the emptiness that filled his heart. I was afraid that he might blame me for the loss of the child, decide to seek a son with another wife instead, as was his right, but his warmth and his kindness for me as his only wife made me feel strong again. We would keep trying and, if the gods thought us worthy, we would have the son he needed if he was to leave his kingdom secure when his time came.

In every other way we were happy. We had not been separated for one night since we were joined in marriage, and I had never for one moment doubted that we were meant to be together. Since the day that we first met, when we were just children, I suppose that the gods had decided we would be as one so I could not understand why they would deny us this happiness and take our unborn children from us. They would have a reason, of course, and we were not to question them. We just had to prove to them that we were worthy for our line to continue. After all, why should it not? My husband was the son of a great king who had died serving his people. Why should the gods not think us worthy?

I missed my mother and my father, especially now, and I know that my husband missed his mother and Rusa. He had become close to this man who had won his mother's heart and I think he almost looked upon him as a father figure. They certainly all seemed very content when they were together. My husband had hoped that Rusa would stay to command his ships, and his mother would then be close, but Rusa had responsibilities of his own on the great island and Kia would not be apart from him again. And so they had gone back, to be closer also to Kitane and Itaja, I think. Their lives were now far away from us and we could only wish them happiness and pray that they would not forget us. We had letters, of course, and we planned visits, but news took a long time to travel and visits had to be organised far in advance, and then plans so often changed at the last minute. If ever people envy the lives of those in power, and who seem to live lives of luxury and privilege, they should remember that, really, we are just the same as them, with many of the same problems, the same fears, and we shed the same tears. Our privileges are bought at a price and we pay it where they cannot see us cry.

But we are soon to begin a journey to another land, far away to the south, beyond the great cataracts that guard our country, and I am excited that my beloved husband may regain something of the joy he has always had for this wonderful land. New sights, new adventures, these may re-awaken in him the passion that seems to have faded recently. He still comes to me as he has always done, but many nights we just lie quietly together. He wonders if he should hold back in case I suffer another heart-breaking loss. I sense he is confused about the message the gods are sending and has an inner struggle to make sense of it. But I will tell him that he is all that I wish for, and if the gods have decided that he must seek an heir from another wife, then I will understand. As long as I do not lose him. That is all I care about.

Huya

He was my king and I loved him, but I was concerned that he was sometimes too trusting, too innocent perhaps. He had come to the throne as just a child, and had reigned in a time of peace and prosperity, his enemies vanquished, his armies powerful. His navy too, under the command of my dearest friend Amasis, a brother from struggles long past, and brother of the late king. My Lord Kamose was still young, something of a dreamer. He always wanted to see the good in people. He had become more withdrawn recently, I had noticed, since the loss of his unborn child, the second son the gods had denied to him, and I wondered if his judgement had been affected. It was as though he wrestled with some inner turmoil, some demon that only he could see. He was worried for his beloved wife, of course, but even she seemed not to know how to reach him. My own wife, Yrsa, was close to the queen and spent time with her every day, as did Amaja who was staying with us in the capital while her husband Amasis was far away with his beloved ships. They gave her the support she needed, but they could see that the only way for Kamose and Reja to be as they were before would be for them to have a child of their own. We were concerned that the king would take another wife, out of desperation not from love, and that a child born to her, as successor to the throne of the two lands, would push the king and his queen yet further apart. This would destroy her and we loved her so much we could not bear this to be the way forward for our land. The king needed a son, we could only pray that the gods would reconsider their judgement and allow Reja to give him one.

Meanwhile we had plans to make for the visit to our neighbour to the south. I had met his father some years before, a good man who valued his friendship with us and the benefits it gave to both our nations. I had also met his son, at least his eldest son, who was to be his successor, and had formed a favourable opinion of him as well. I was not then aware that there was another, younger, son, and would have had no thought that it would be this one who would be king after the old man died. We had been given some idea as to how this came about, but even I found the explanation difficult to believe. I know that Nehsi, the senior commander of my king's armies and a beloved friend, believed it even less. But Kamose was happy to make the visit, to travel to another land beyond the safety of his own borders, and meet another king. He loved to travel and the idea itself was a good one, to distract him perhaps from some of his other worries, but both Nehsi and I were concerned that he might underestimate the risks involved. We would use the council meeting later in the morning to try to persuade him, gently, that a show of force would have a greater benefit at the start of this new king's reign than gifts of gold and silver. Some gifts, yes, but take the opportunity to remind Tarka that we were not to be taken lightly. The enormous forts that had been built beyond the first of the great cataracts that guarded our southern borders were now old and had not been fully manned for many generations. They had fallen into disrepair and were used as customs posts and storage centres rather than garrisons. I know that Nehsi had given orders to have the walls repaired and to have supplies and men sent south to reinforce their ability to withstand a siege. One of these would be our base for the first part of the visit and, perhaps, our refuge if something should go wrong and we be tricked, even attacked. We had no wish or reason to antagonise our new neighbour but, equally, it would do no harm to make him realise that we took our security very seriously.

Nehsi

I was pleased that the king seemed more focussed at the council meeting and listened with care to the arguments that I, and my deputy Huya, placed before him. He was enthusiastic about the visit to King Tarka, he had not travelled so far from his southern borders before, but we were concerned that he may have lost some of his usual caution. I think we managed to convince him that, while the trip may be enormously valuable for trade and for ensuring we maintained good relations with a useful ally, there was always the possibility that we may be being lured into danger. We managed to persuade him that more troops should be included in the party without actually specifying a number. The king may have thought in terms of tens, I was thinking more in terms of thousands. Coming to the throne as just a young child, His Majesty had never served in the army and had little military experience. He had seen his vast army at manoeuvre, of course, and had led mock chariot charges across rolling desert sands, but he had never experienced combat and had never seen blood spilled in battle. I fear he was more of a dreamer than a schemer, and believed that there was good in everyone. We all loved him but we were more cautious in our advice to him, trying to draw attention to the subplots he perhaps did not even realise could be there. I planned to spice up this visit by holding extensive wargames in the hills and deserts closer to the southern borders, encouraging His Majesty to observe and, perhaps, even take part in, a wide range of mock battles. I planned for Amasis to have a number of different river vessels to convey us as far as the first cataract, and for Huya to demonstrate what his specialist archers could do in the complex terrain of the deserts and hills. All of this would provide valuable training for troops too long idle, and it would do no harm for our prospective host to learn, via his inevitable spies, just what we were capable of. And, most of all, we would have a vast army to hand should we need them.

I took the opportunity also to have the great forts along the river beyond the cataracts repaired and their garrisons restored. These had been raised by kings long ago, and had served in the past to demonstrate our might and power to neighbouring kings and warlords themselves long departed. Now, sadly, they were crumbling and their store rooms of grain and weapons were long depleted. But by time we arrive they should be at least better able to serve as a base suitable for a king and his party. I was also a little concerned that the king intended to take his young wife along but I knew it was pointless to object. They went everywhere together and had done so since they were married as little more than children. She was a beautiful young woman, truly loved by all who met her, and I would willingly give my life to protect her, but I prayed that she might be with child when we came to depart and would stay behind where she could be better cared for.

Reja

I must confess that even I was becoming caught up in the excitement of the coming journey south and the visit to our exotic neighbour. I was well familiar with some of the products of his lands, at least from the time of his father, and marvelled at some of the animal skins we had received. What wondrous beasts must live in those parts. And the spices and oils that we traded for and which filled our palaces with their wondrous aromas. One of my servant girls, Takami, had been a gift from the old king, and she was easily the most beautiful and intimate of my companions. She had the darkest and smoothest skin, and a smile that could cheer my whole day. I made sure that she would accompany us and I was determined that if she truly wished to remain behind in her own land afterwards, then I would allow it. I would miss her, and the intimate massages which she gave me that made me feel so wonderfully relaxed, but if I could make her happy by such a simple gesture then I would do it. We were about the same age and had shared so many secrets that I had come to think of her far more as a friend than as a servant, and never as a slave. She had seemed a little uncertain when I told her that I wanted her with me, I thought she would be glad of the chance to visit her homeland again, but I knew she would not let me down. I could command it, of course, but I would not think of making her come against her wishes. We would have time to talk about it, when my husband was otherwise engaged with matters of planning with his staff, and I would find out why she had hesitated.

There were signs that the journey was soon to begin as more and more ships arrived at the capital to transport troops and supplies upstream. I had heard that there would be army manoeuvres at the same time, something I knew my husband would enjoy watching, and that he was enthusiastic that Amasis would be taking charge of the enormous flotilla. He dearly loved his uncle, as did I, but I was a little sad that neither Yrsa nor Amaja would be coming with us, or their children. It seemed that royal protocol discouraged so many members of the family being away from the capital together for so long, or at least that was what Huya told me. Anyway, I was greatly looking forward to having my husband to myself for so long as we made our way to the south. The journey up river would take many days, and there would be many nights lying peacefully at anchor, and we would be away for many weeks in total. I was determined to be with child again when we returned.

Kamose

Of course I knew what he was up to. The cunning old fox, did he really think that I didn't know that the manoeuvres were planned just so that we could arrive in the south with a huge army and yet not arouse too many suspicions from our host? But I also knew how seriously my generals took the security of our borders, and I would not override their wisdom or their experience. I may have limited military experience myself, but I hope I am not so stupid as to ignore theirs!

I decided that I would undertake one journey first for myself, to the north, to the old capital, while preparations were underway here. I had to talk to Teti before we left. I would return with Amasis as he made his way upriver with the last of the ships from the marsh areas that boarded the sea. On this occasion I decided I would not take Reja with me. I needed time to consider our situation, and I could not do so clearly when she was so close to my thoughts and my arms. It would only be a week or so, but we had not spent a single night apart since we were married. I prayed that she would understand and not read into the act something that was not there. I left Huya to begin the movement of the men, and especially the enormous number of chariots and wagons that could not use the river, on their long journey south into the deserts. They would travel via the chain of lakes that offered fertile land among the sands and would need time to reach their destination before us. Nehsi would wait for me in the capital and we would travel south together, with Amasis and his remaining ships, when everything was in order. I took only a small staff to the north with me, and my usual bodyguard. I felt no need of guards but I had long been told that it was tradition and as much for ceremony as protection. In truth, what I wanted most from the journey to the old capital was to be alone with my thoughts.

Teti

It would be so good to see the king again. I had wondered if, when I returned to the north, he would still want my council let alone my company. We had agreed that another vizier, perhaps two, would need to be appointed and I had selected several promising men for his consideration. I was happy to retire from my post, the years were taking their toll and travelling especially was becoming more of a challenge. The problem was that I felt exactly the same on the inside as I had those many years ago when I had first become deputy to the man I had loved as a brother, who had been vizier of this great land for so long, and whose company and council I missed more than I would ever have believed. On the outside, though, I certainly no longer looked or felt the same. Aches and stiffness that sometimes prevented me even mounting a horse that I could once have ridden all day, and a lack of clarity in my vision, especially when reading documents in poorly formed script, all made me realise I was so much closer now to the end than to the beginning. And, most regretful of all, I could no longer fully enjoy the pleasures of the two most wonderful women I had ever known, now my beloved wives. At least, not as often or for as long as before.

And now the king was coming to see me, before undertaking his visit to the kingdom beyond our southern borders. But I had the feeling from his message that it was not this royal visit that was troubling him, that he wanted to talk to me about something else entirely. I had heard he was troubled, distracted even, not just with mourning the loss of his unborn children. I knew how much he loved his wife, the queen, and perhaps shared his concern at what might be felt by the people if she lost another child in the future. The people needed to know that the king had an heir. Order required it. A smooth succession, even if the throne passed to a child, was preferable to dynastic conflict as others sought to rule by force of arms.

On the day that he arrived we all went down to the dock to greet him. The ceremonies were mercifully short, the king was clearly tired from his journey. In public the king's person was sacred, not to be touched, but in the privacy of our own palace we hugged. We were family and this was something that we did without even a second thought. Kashta and Nefret fussed over him, and he presented each of them with some exquisite fragrant oils that he had instructed be made especially for them from the flowers in the palace gardens. He embraced me warmly and I felt that he genuinely wanted my council. I suggested we walk in the gardens, alongside the river, where we could talk in private.

As we walked he unburdened himself, slowly at first, almost hesitantly, and then in a torrent. How he knew that the last king, Senwasre, was not his true father, that he had known there was something that his mother had tried to hide from him but, at the same time, clearly wanted him to know. And then, the realisation that his father was still alive and was the man his mother so clearly and dearly loved. Then, coming to love and respect Rusa as a man he was proud to know as his father, although the world must not know it. Chaos would follow if it became known he was not the son, the true heir, of the last king. And that, perhaps, the loss of his unborn sons was the gods telling him that the succession was not certain until he had proved himself worthy, a king in his own right. There was so much that he had been holding inside, so much that had preoccupied him over the last months. He swore me to absolute secrecy, of course, but there was no need. He knew that nothing that passed between us in confidence would ever escape my lips. But so it was that I was finally able to unburden myself of a secret I too had kept, burning into my soul, for so many years. That I had already guessed, and so had Senwasre.

The king had realised how convenient it had been that Kia had born a son so soon after her return from the great island, and how Kitane had also born a child soon after her marriage to another man. This thought, that there had been another man in his beloved wife's arms, pained him greatly and he was very observant to the child, more even than any other doting father. As he came to suspect that the child may not be his own, he confided his fears in me and we spoke, as we are doing now, in secret and at great length. He was hurt, of course, desperately hurt, but he could say nothing or risk losing his beloved wife. I was able to remind him that it did not matter if Kamose was not his true son, that he himself had not been the true son of the previous king, but that the king had adopted him when he married his mother and had loved him and had treated him in every way as his son. He could adopt Kamose as his son and heir, if the deception troubled him, and this would be perfectly acceptable to the gods and to the people. And we both agreed that there was absolutely no suggestion that Kamose would not be a good king when his time came. There was just one, simple problem. To adopt the boy and confirm him as his rightful heir it would be necessary to acknowledge that he was not the boy's true father, otherwise there would be no need for the adoption. And that, in turn, would tell the world that the boy's mother had been unfaithful to him. This was what he could not face. And so it had not been done. With his premature death in battle, the dilemma had now passed to the shoulders of Kamose himself. Should he acknowledge that he was not the true son of the last king and risk being declared a usurper, try for a son with another wife and risk losing the woman he truly loved, or hope that the gods would keep his secret and, hopefully, forgive him if he could just prove himself worthy. The issue of the succession now ate away at Kamose until he could not rest, just as it had eaten away at Senwasre. And so, as we walked, we considered the future of his reign.

Reja

I finally learned her secret, late one warm night, when we had exhausted each other with our growing love and lay naked on the bed together in the darkness, trying to cool down. I had been angry that my husband had not taken me with him to the north, I would like to have seen Teti and his family as well. This was the first time we had spent our nights apart since we were joined in marriage, and I had no hesitation in asking Takami to comfort me in his place. She had come to me willingly, anxious, I think, to talk about the journey ahead. And so, as we relaxed in the darkness, she told me. She had been a gift to us from her father, this I knew, along with other valuable items to celebrate our marriage and to reinforce the alliance between his kingdom and our own. She had not been a slave, just intended as a servant for the royal household. She had been young and lonely but had been made welcome and treated well so she had not really missed her home. Anyway, she had not got on well there with her twin brother and had been relieved to be freed from his bullying attention. She had loved her father, and her elder brother, but they had been so busy with their own lives that little time had been available for her. So she had become part of a new family, and had become first my personal servant, then my childhood companion, then my friend, and now my lover. She did not substitute for my beloved husband, of course, but we were comfort for each other when days, and sometimes nights, were lonely. She had heard that her father had died, he was an old man so this was less of a shock than it might have been, but then her older brother was also taken from her in mysterious and tragic circumstances. And at the heart of everything, there was her twin brother, manipulating all around him and eventually taking his elder brother's place. I looked at her wide-eyed as the story began to make more sense to me. Her twin brother was Tarka, the very man we were travelling south to visit in a matter of weeks. She was the daughter of the last king and the sister of the present king. My dearest friend was a princess!

So, now I understood why she hesitated to accompany me on the journey south. I eventually managed to persuade her, and we were both exhausted and glistening with the effort. I assured her that, since my husband would be very busy during the visit, I would be far too lonely without her, and so she agreed she would come. But she pleaded with me to tell no-one, not even the king, of her secret, and she gave me a sombre warning. Her brother was not to be trusted.

The following days were busy as the ships that would take us south gradually arrived and we all began the lengthy process of embarkation. I ran down to the dock to welcome Kamose as soon as I heard his ship, Amasis's ship, was approaching, and I was ashamed at my anger with him when he embraced me so warmly in front of everyone and with no regard for protocol. The look in his eyes when he saw me removed any doubt I may have had that I had in some way slipped from his affection. It was good to see Amasis as well, he had been such a support for us both over the years. We made our way back to the palace for the king to deliver his final instructions to his ministers. His new vizier was to be confirmed in office later in the day, he was from a good family and came well recommended, and he had been observed by both the king and by Teti for many months. They were both confident that he would serve the king well. Meanwhile, since we would be gone for many months, the king had to make clear how he wished his kingdom to be run in his absence. We also wanted a few more hours together as a family. Amasis had not seen his wife and son for many months and we were sensitive to their needs as well. We would leave with the morning mists still on the river and begin our laborious passage south against the flow of the great river. I was so excited.

PART 2

Amasis

It was all I could do to appear calm as I brought the great ship close to the dock and made her secure. My eyes scanned the crowd for the two faces above all I longed to see, my beloved wife Amaja and my son Senwasre. There was much bustle, and a large crowd had gathered to welcome the king, but I could not see them. I quickly became swept up in the ceremonies of the disembarkation and the supervision of the other ships already docked and preparing to leave on our great mission. The king went off with his own wife for meetings at the palace and I followed shortly afterwards, having been embraced in a most affectionate way by the queen. It is a delight to see how often the king and queen ignore protocol when greeting their true friends and family. It does not diminish in any way the respect the people have for them, if anything it only seems to make the people love them more.

She was waiting for me in the gardens of the palace, along with Senwasre and Yrsa with her daughter Akila. The children had been playing together and were hot and dusty. It was a delight to embrace them all after so long apart and I was only sad that that I could not take my wife completely into my arms there and then. We swapped a look that promised much for later and then we all went down to the great pool at the end of the garden to swim and cool down. Since I had experienced more than enough water recently, I chose to sit in the shade with some most welcome refreshments while the others played. None of them had the slightest inhibition about stripping off their clothes, and the sight of both my wife and the wife of my best friend, naked and laughingly splashing each other with the cold water, was uncomfortably arousing. It was clear that Amaja and Yrsa were very fond of each other, they must have been lonely during the many days and nights that Huya and I spent away from them on the king's business, and I felt comforted that, perhaps, they had each other for when the nights seemed longest and loneliest.

Even little Akila was showing the first signs of becoming a woman. Her hair and skin were a little darker than her mother's, but there was no doubt that she was going to be a very beautiful woman, just like her mother. How time was moving on. I noticed the attention that my son was paying to her and thought that, since children are often betrothed at such a young age, this was perhaps something we should discuss when Huya and I returned and we were all together again. They obviously liked each other and it would be a good match. And so my mind wandered as everyone else played, and the next thing I knew I was being awakened by a cold, wet, laughing mouth being pressed against my own.

There was a banquet later in the day, after a ceremony to install the new vizier now that Teti had formally retired, and there were many speeches and prayers for the success of the visit to the kingdom of our southern neighbour. And then, finally, Amaja and I could be alone. It had been so long since we had held each other and my longing for her quite overwhelmed me. It was many hours later when we finally slept.

Now it was time. The last of the enormous river craft cast off into the mist that lingered on the water, and with oars and some sail we manoeuvred ourselves into the middle of the great river. Leaving space for each boat to keep clear of the others, we began to move south to our great adventure. The king and the queen travelled with me, accompanied by the queen's companion who I hardly recognised. She had been just a gangly girl the last time I had seen her, with a mischievous smile and great sense of fun, but now, like the queen herself, she had grown into a most beautiful young woman. The two were obviously very close. The queen had insisted that the king's staff and ministers travelled on other boats, even sending Nehsi to travel on another vessel, albeit with a nudge and a wink which he smilingly understood. We would meet up with them when we anchored for the night, of course, but I think she wanted her husband to herself during the days ahead. Although we had to be cautious moving around some of the larger islands, and where the river shallowed with great and unpredictable sand banks, the sailing was largely uneventful and the voyage was most pleasant. At one point the king thought of trying to harpoon one of the enormous animals that wallowed close to the bank, its tusks were the size of a man's arm, but the queen urged him to show mercy, that the magnificent animal was clearly a mother with a calf close by, and the king smiled and laid down his weapon. He would do nothing that would upset his beautiful young wife and I felt happy for the love they obviously shared. This made me think of Reja's mother, Kitane, and then of Kia, both now settled into their own lives far to the north across the great sea, and I felt a deep sadness at how much I missed them all. We had shared so many adventures.

But my eye was caught by the sailing master of the ship who wanted to change the tack of the enormous vessel as the river began to narrow. In truth, his knowledge of the river far exceeded my own, my world was with the tides and currents of the great seas far to the north, but I was commander of all of the king's ships and all captain's looked to me for their orders. A nod was all it took to let this good man use his own judgement and the ship slowly began to turn. Another few days and we would arrive at our destination. I began to wonder what my role would be then in this particular adventure. I would never have been able to guess what lay ahead for us all in the future.

Kamose

It had been good to speak with Teti. His calmness, his wise council. Although I was surprised that he knew my secret, I suppose I should have expected it. If I had worked things out then, of course, he who was so much wiser than me would have done so as well. I started to wonder if anyone else had thought the same but then reasoned that no-one else would have any reason to even consider the matter. No, my secret was safe, of that I was sure. But he gave me comfort and that was why I had travelled so far to see him.

The journey home with Amasis gave us much time to relax and talk about family and friends. He talked of my parents, and told me things about my mother I had not known. About how brave she had been on so many occasions, often alone and so far from home, about pirates and battles, and more about the wonderful friendship she had with Kitane and how much they both loved my father, Senwasre. Many of the tales I had heard before, of course, but there were always extra details and I loved to hear them again. They brought family close when they were so far away. I managed to slip in questions about Rusa as well, casually, anxious to know more about the man who was my true father from those who had known him in his other life, before he had married my mother. I began to realise how little I knew about those I loved so much, and how rich their lives had been.

But when we finally arrived back at the capital, all other feelings were swept away in my happiness at seeing Reja again. We had not been apart for so long before, not since we were children, and I realised how very much I never wanted to be apart from her again. She seemed anxious when we first embraced, I think she was still uncertain if my time away had been to discuss with Teti whether I should seek a new wife to safeguard the succession, and I made sure that she was reassured that no-one else would ever come between us. Meanwhile, there were ceremonies to attend to and banquets were being organised, we would be busy before our flotilla would be ready to depart in just a few days. The ships had to be resupplied and repaired, men and equipment had to be embarked, final plans agreed for how we would travel and where and when we would meet up again before our arrival at the great cataracts that marked the end of the river and the southern border of my kingdom. But first I had to have time with Reja and I had to have time to wash the fatigue of travel from my aching bones.

We left Amasis to join his own family and eventually managed to usher the servants and officials out of our apartments, to be alone at last, if only until the evening. Most of all I wanted to bathe, at leisure, without someone having to keep a watch for crocodiles or hippos, and then I wanted to be massaged with soothing oils. I longed to smell like a king again and not like a deckhand on a riverboat! Normally such personal attention would be given by a servant, but Reja had long-ago taken on all responsibilities for my physical welfare. It was a luxury beyond compare to sink with her into the enormous tub that we had in our private quarters, and be washed and then massaged by the most beautiful girl in my entire kingdom. Perhaps I was biased but to me there was no competition. And I had not fully appreciated how being apart from her for so long would make it impossible for me not to show her solid evidence of just how much I wanted and needed her. Several times.

The most important ceremony I had to perform before we departed was to install my new vizier, a man of middle years named Ramose, in his mighty office. This man would be my voice in so many matters and my chief counsellor. He had fulfilled many lesser roles over the years and had been carefully watched as he met with ambassadors, made judgements in the courts, and supervised great projects across the lands. Teti had expressed himself satisfied and I trusted Teti above all men. Ramose was duly appointed my vizier and endowed with the appropriate chains and staff of office. He seemed to swell with pride almost to the point of bursting. I almost smiled at his new, regal, air, but I happened to catch the eye of Nehsi standing quietly to one side. He did not bow as the others did, as chief of all of my armies he was the equal of the vizier and did not bow to him, but the look on his face flashed a warning that quite surprised me. He clearly did not trust this man and he was telling me, as loudly as a look could tell, that I should be careful. Suddenly, the pompous little man in front of me did not seem quite so amusing.

Reja

The voyage was all that I had hoped it would be. The ships were not as grand as those that crossed the great seas to the north, like the ones we had travelled on to the great island to visit Kia and Kitane and their families, but they were grand none-the-less. There was much to do to for the crews to work the sails and the oars, to change tack around the small islands and sandbanks, and there was always something to watch, some new experience to wonder at. And the view changed with every bend and with every new day. Sometimes the tall yellow cliffs seemed to close in around us, silencing everyone on board with almost a sense of awe, none wanting to make any sound which would create an echo which almost made it seem like the gods were speaking to us. At other times the cliffs moved back and stretches of green, productive land would appear, occasionally dotted with small farms where naked men, sometimes whole families, toiled in the fields. This was, indeed, a most wonderful land. There were other boats ahead of us, others behind, and I saw people occasionally on the banks as we passed look at us with open mouths. This was probably something that none of them had ever seen before and would be a tale told to their families for years to come. I stood with my husband the king as his lands drifted past and felt that my life was complete. I even forgot, for a while, what had made me so sad for so long. But I did not forget what I had intended to do about it.

When it became dark, when the sandbanks could not be seen clearly and the ships could not be sailed safely, we tied up for the night. Sometimes we landed at temples and were made welcome by the small groups of priests that served the gods that dwelt there, but more often we just tied up at the bank, the ships anchored against rocks or trees or even against great stakes driven into the deep black mud. Guards were posted, fires were lit, and it would not be long before the smell of food wafted through the air and the sounds of singing came from the many small camps set up along the riverside. And night after night I showed my husband how much I loved him and how much I needed him.

A king has many duties, of course, and is never completely at leisure. He had meetings with ministers and secretaries, with

Nehsi and his senior commanders, with Amasis and his captains. There were plans to make for when we arrived at our final destination, messages to be sent overland to his army camped, we hoped, somewhere ahead of us in the desert, messages to be sent and received from the vizier via riders who followed us along the banks, sometimes for many hours. It was when he was busy with these matters that I shared my time with Takami. She knew how busy I was when my husband was with me but she also knew that there were many lonely hours in my day as well. And I did not want her to feel that she had no place in my life when my husband was around. On one such late afternoon, when the ships were anchored where the river became particularly narrow and we had decided to wait until the full light of the following morning before travelling further, and when Kamose was ashore at yet another meeting, Takami came to our cabin with fragrant oils to soothe my tensions away. We were close now to our destination and I knew that the king would soon have so much to do that I would, once again, see him only rarely. I could not even depend on our nights together for a while since he would be watching and supervising his wargames in the desert which could take him away from me for days at a time. And Takami herself was clearly anxious at approaching her own homeland and the uncertain welcome she would receive from her brother, the new king. She wanted to know in detail what had happened when her father died and why her elder brother had not been crowned king, but she was afraid that answers would not be forthcoming and that lies and deceit would confirm her worst fears. So she massaged me and freed me of tensions and I did the same for her. It was at this point, when we were both naked and her glistening body was beneath me as I knelt over her face, her tongue working busily to give me pleasure and both of us oblivious to our surroundings, that I suddenly looked up to see Kamose in the doorway staring at us.

Nehsi

I don't know why I distrusted my king's new vizier so much, but I did. There was something in his manner that made me feel uncomfortable in a way that I had never felt with Teti. Teti made everyone feel comfortable, worthy, and no-one I had ever come across had spoken ill of him. Even if I disagreed with his decisions I always understood why he had made them and freely acknowledge that, usually, it turned out that he had been right and I had been wrong. But this Ramose, he was different. I tried to sound out other opinions, to see if I was being unreasonable, but none that I spoke to had seen enough of him to doubt the king's decision. I would have to mind my own council, for now at least. But there was one thing I could do and I left instructions with trusted men back in the capital to send me messages if there was anything that they felt I should know about. These I could compare with messages received by the king from the vizier and see, perhaps, if he was being told the whole story.

Anyway, for now there were other matters to occupy me. Our final destination was in sight and I could only admire the way that the ships were brought around, one by one, to anchor safely against the banks near the enormous cataracts that marked the end of the easy passage along the great river. There were men and supplies to unload, officers and old friends to greet, and an enormous camp to establish. Huya had arrived some time before with most of the army, though there were others still arriving almost every day, and we had the men spread out over a wide area so as not to strip the land around of all of its vegetation for our animals. We had supplies in plenty on our ships but it was always a challenge to get the food to the mouths that needed it. Amasis and Huya greeted each other like brothers, and it felt good to be once again with people I had absolute trust in. The men cheered the king as he went among them and there was an atmosphere almost of a great celebration now that we were all finally together. It had taken a lot to coordinate the movement of such an army so far and we were all proud of what they had done. There would be weeks of wargames while some of the lighter boats were dragged through the rapids to the next navigable stretch of the river, and then some would travel on by boat while others would make their way across the desert to meet up with our host for the celebrations to follow. He would send guides for our journey but we all knew that his spies would be watching every move we made in the meantime and reporting back to their master. We would give them something to talk about, that was for sure.

Kamose

I finally managed to finish the meeting with my commanders, with everyone clear about what was needed over the next few days. I missed Reja and decided to surprise her and take her with me to a quiet lunch away from the bustle of the main camp. We would not have many more times to be alone together for a while, and I wanted to be sure she knew how much I loved her before I left her again to be with my army.

The boat was quiet and I assumed she would be sleeping or resting in our cabin. As I approached I was concerned that a soft moaning sound from within suggested she may be ill, and I pushed open the door carefully and peered inside. There was not much light since the small window was shuttered against the intense heat and, at first, I was not sure exactly what I was seeing. But when it became clear that my wife was not alone, and that she was involved in something so intimate, I stood unable to speak. They did not notice me at first and I became lost in the scene before me. I knew Reja was fond of the girl Takami, of course, she followed us everywhere and was a devoted servant and companion, even more like a friend for my wife I think, and I certainly noticed she was very beautiful, but I never imagined for even one moment that she and my wife were almost as married as we were. They continued to give each other intense pleasure, completely unaware of my presence, and I found that I was becoming very aroused by the scene and not angered by it. Reja was a very sensual young woman and often gave loud notice of her pleasure when we were together, but I had never heard her make so much sign that she was so completely lost in herself before. And the position was not one we had ever explored together and I wondered why, since she so obviously enjoyed it. I had almost decided to leave and pretend I had not seen them when, at exactly that moment, she turned her head and our eyes met. She was frozen in horror and made to rise to her feet, her hand over her mouth in shock and shame. The girl Takami, likewise, made to rise and grabbed for her clothes to cover herself. I closed the door behind me and moved towards the bed, trying to show them that I was not angry, only a little surprised. My wife's first thoughts were to assure me that she was not with Takami because I did not satisfy her, only that she was lonely when I was away from her. Takami also seemed more afraid that she had been found being so intimate with the queen whose person was sacred. They both looked scared and I took them into my arms to show them I was not angry. I kissed Reja gently and told them both to sit with me on the bed. I did not hide from them that I had been very aroused by what I had witnessed, and made it clear that we would need to explore this new part of our relationship. And so the afternoon passed rather differently from how I had intended, and Reja and I never did go for our quiet lunch together.

Huya

The cheers were deafening as the king rode between the ranks of the assembled army in his golden chariot. It was the first day of the wargames and the excitement was building. At first there would be parades, showing drill and the ability of so many men to march and turn together at the commands of trumpets and drums. This would spread everyone out over the vast desert plane and create space for the chariot races to follow. These had originally been planned as mock attacks but it soon became clear that the men would treat them as races anyway and so they had developed. Teams would race each other, and then groups of chariots would race together, the next one only starting when the previous one had completed a circuit. Every skill of horsemanship and chariotry would be tested, and the cheers of the men would help to bring out the best of skills in men and horses alike. The king had wanted to compete as well but Nehsi and I finally managed to persuade him that the dangers would be too great to risk. Nehsi swung the argument by suggesting that, since no-one would dare to beat the king in a race anyway, the games would be unfair and so less exciting to watch. His majesty was not persuaded by so obvious a lie, given anyway with an enormous wink to me, but he conceded that his presence in the race might be more of a distraction than a benefit.

By the end of the first day the horses were exhausted, the men hardly able any longer to speak from cheering, and so much gold had been awarded in prizes that some of the champions looked more like a king than the king himself. Everyone had enjoyed a magnificent day and there were feasts in every one of the many camps. The king went from fire to fire, talking with his men, congratulating winners, cheering those that had tried so hard, and, as night fell and the darkness enveloped us all, I looked out over an army that would have defied the gods themselves if their king had asked them to. There would be more contests over the coming days, in javelins and archery, in armed and unarmed combat, and in climbing and fighting among the many hills that surrounded us, but for the moment I could not have been more proud of the men we had with us. I tried to find the king to see if he had any orders for the night, I was technically his chief body guard after all, but he was nowhere to be found. A sentry told me that he had seemed to be in a hurry to return to the quarters which he shared with his wife and her beautiful companion, on the largest of the boats moored on the river. I did not disturb him. He deserved his rest, it had been a magnificent day.

Amasis

I quite envied Huya playing at soldiers away on the sands, and was frequently distracted by the loud sounds of cheering that came from that area. My tasks were somewhat harder. We could not take the large ships that had brought us here any further.

The rapids and narrows made the passage of such large vessels impossible. We could dismantle them, of course, but that was a task that would have taken even longer and required more specialised craftsmen than we had with us. But we had several smaller boats that would fit in the narrow channels and which could be hauled through the crashing water to the calmer river beyond. All it would take would be a lot of men pulling very hard for several days. Nothing really!

By the end of the first day we had worked out the best way to handle the ropes and to allow the men to rest, briefly, between bouts of labour. We anchored the ropes against bronze spikes driven into gaps between the rocks and this made the efforts of the teams pulling on the ropes much easier. The first boat took us most of the first day, but by the end of the second day we had hauled up another two. The men were exhausted and made their camps gratefully as darkness fell. Another two days and we should have moved enough of the smaller boats to allow passage to the next of the great cataracts. Then we had to carry up the supplies they would need and check that none of the boats needed any repairs. I did not know this part of the river, indeed I had only once before travelled this far to the south, but I had men with me who knew the area well and they had drawn pictures in the sand to show me the land that was ahead of us. We had to establish our main base at the largest of the rebuilt fortresses just before the next enormous set of rapids and narrow channels, but that would be many more days sailing away. Most of the army would remain here. I know that Nehsi wanted to be sure we had an army close by in case we should need it, but the king and his closest bodyguard would travel into the southern kingdom of our host under his protection. Armies from our lands had been this way in the past, led by kings whose accomplishments and conquests were legendary, but we were at peace with these lands now and entering with too large an army could be seen as provocative. It was a delicate balance.

The following morning, just as the men were getting ready to begin their labours, the king came to see our progress and to cheer the men on. He passed among them, spoke to even the humblest sailors, and made sure that none with injuries were being forced to work until they were recovered. It is strange that kings can be distant, mighty figures, who inspire awe in their subjects, or just like ordinary men, who walk among their subjects and show they care for them. I would not suggest for one moment that our king, for all of his lack of pomp and ceremony, was loved any less than the most legendary heroes. Kingship comes from within, it is not simply gifted by the wearing of a crown. It may, of course, have helped that the king did not make his morning inspection alone. The queen was an absolute favourite with all of the men, I'm sure every one of them would have died for her, and she was every bit their sister as much as she was their queen. One man, who had been feigning a leg injury to avoid some of the heavier labour, actually sprang to his feet as she approached so as not to be passed by and overlooked. The overseer gave him a glare that almost guaranteed he would never play such a trick again!

And so the day passed, and the next, in unrelenting labour. But we succeeded magnificently and secured enough boats above the wild rapids to allow the king and his party to proceed upstream to the great fort which would his base. The wargames had also progressed well and the king had taken part in chariot charges at the head of his army just as I knew he had hoped to do. The mock battles, excuses for advanced training second only to real warfare, would continue for a while longer to prevent the men from feeling idle and to ensure the new recruits were well embedded into their units for whatever may lie ahead. Huya would remain with the main army while Nehsi would accompany us to the south. His seniority would give the appropriate formality to our delegation since the vizier had to remain behind in the capital. We would be much reduced in number but the guides from our host, King Tarka, had already arrived to conduct the main part of the king's bodyguard across the desert to join us at the fort. At the last moment, Nehsi announced that he would prefer to travel across the desert with his men rather than accompany us on the water, there was still something making him unsettled, and the king, respecting the judgement of his chief general, reluctantly agreed. We, at least, would have a restful few days on the still mighty river as we made our way ever further into the fiery cauldron of the south. To what adventures, however, none of us could possibly have imagined.

PART 3

Nehsi

I had received only a single message from my agents in the capital, and nothing was reported to me that was in any way suspicious. The new vizier was, it seemed, conducting the business of state perfectly appropriately and there were no rumours or accounts of unusual activities that I could focus on. The king received far more reports but these, again, were routine and unremarkable. He passed them to me as a courtesy but I could read nothing into them to justify my still nagging feeling that, for some reason, all was not well.

The wargames went well, better in fact than I expected, and it was a real pleasure to see how the men behaved in the presence of their king and how well and enthusiastically they followed him into battle. I was also impressed at what a natural leader he was showing himself to be. There was no pomp or ceremony other than was necessary, and he genuinely seemed as happy to join his men around a makeshift fire and share their simple food as sit at an extravagant banquet. He had never had any real chance to be a soldier before but he was showing now that his father's blood ran through him. And Senwasre had been a great soldier, his time cut brutally short by a coward striking him from behind on a remote stretch of sand far from home.

The boats had been hauled above the rapids, and we did not doubt how hard a task this must have been, and Amasis was supervising the loading of the king's party and his senior staff in the calmer waters beyond. Almost as I was about to join them I had another feeling that something was not well. The guides had arrived from Tarka and they would lead the bodyguard, whose numbers I had surreptitiously managed to increase, through the sands to the fortress which I had instructed to be prepared for us, but I hesitated to leave my men totally in their care. I was, perhaps, the only one in the king's party who had any knowledge of this desert region and I was anxious to see just how much these guides could be trusted. I obtained the king's permission, given reluctantly I could see, and pretending no knowledge of the area at all, I prepared to join the remainder of the army on its move south. We left most of the men and most of the chariots and wagons behind, under Huya's command, but I was confident they could be summoned if they were needed.

The three guides claimed no knowledge of our language and seemed a surly little group. I was unable, therefore, to question them about our route or even how long the journey might take. They even seemed unable to understand simple gestures and I began to feel that their stupidity was assumed rather than real and they had been instructed to say nothing. They remained together at all times, declined to share our fires or our food, and only spoke among themselves in a tongue I found incomprehensible. But I could tell from the movement of the sun in the sky and the position of the lanterns in the sky at night that they were not taking us directly to where I expected us to go. We were making an enormous loop away from the river across ground that did not seem to offer any easier or safer passage and which seemed unremarkable in every way. I instructed my officers to keep a sharp watch at night and to ration the water carefully. Although the purpose of the guides was supposedly to ensure our safe passage, via wells and valleys that offered shade and refreshment, so far we had found neither water nor shelter. It began to seem that we were being taken further into the desert to reduce our water and to weaken us from the extreme heat. I decided that I would allow them one further day to prove that they were honest in their actions, and then I would have to risk our entire mission by binding our guides and altering our march in what I felt absolutely sure was a more correct direction. I was increasingly concerned for the king as well. What was this southern king, Tarka, planning if he wanted the king's bodyguard to be kept safely out of the way? And if the king was in danger, how could I possibly warn him?

Teti

Rumours. There were always rumours. I seemed to have spent so much of my life listening to and appraising rumours. But how often had there been some truth in them? I had been enjoying my retirement. I had discovered fishing in the marshes near to my home, and many days were spent happily in a small reed boat rowed along by my servant, almost as old as me and a friend of many years far more than just a servant, trailing a line for the evening's meal. I caught little it is true, and much of what I did catch would hardly have fed a small cat let alone a family, but the pleasure was great indeed. And the pleasures of spending more time with my beloved wives, Kashta and Nefret, meant that I lacked for nothing. My heart was at peace. And then came the rumours.

I could not have been vizier of this great land for so long without a network of spies and agents. I learned this from my predecessor, Kashta's late father, and a man I loved and respected above all others. There was nothing sinister here, these were not men who peered into other men's secrets or brought terror to the night, but normal people, shopkeepers, servants, traders, who watched and listened and reported back on what people were worried about and where corruption made good people's lives difficult. Often there would just be a single tale of bad service from an official or strange goings on at a border crossing, easily remedied, but, occasionally, multiple reports from different people would tell a darker story. And so it was here. And, at the centre of so many reports, was my successor as vizier, Ramose. Reports hesitated to criticise, some of the events seemed so trivial my agents said, but his behaviour was being widely seen as causing concern. There were secret meetings where experienced ministers were excluded, decisions being taken which should have been discussed further with the king, mysterious figures seen around the palace whose identity the guards were told not to question. I paced the gardens of my own home becoming deeply concerned. The king was far away and so was his army. The borders were secure, the king would not have travelled so far from home if this was in any doubt, but a vizier had the power to move armies and to open or close borders. He should act always for the king, of course, but his seal was enough to change the destiny of the land if he chose to do so. And if the king was far away, there was no-one to stop him. But what could I do to challenge him? I no longer even had an official boat to take me to the southern capital and could not guarantee that, even if I went, I would be granted an audience. I could see the king without even knocking on his door, but that was a courtesy and not a right. Here, I had nothing. But I would have to go. And take my chances. I still had friends at court. I would visit Amaja and Yrsa and the children. We would all go, make a holiday of it. And I would try to see for myself if the rumours were true.

Reja

The heat was greater than anything I had known before, more than anywhere else I had travelled to. There was nowhere to escape from the stifling air. Occasionally, when the boat was moving, the wind across the water was blissfully cooling but more often we just moved through hot air. The boat was much smaller than the one that had brought us to the first of the rapids and now we had only a small cabin. It was too hot to sleep in there so we used it only to store our clothes and slept on deck with the crew, behind a small screen to have a little privacy. And there was far too little privacy for anything intimate.

I was devastated to have been discovered by my husband when I was in such an intimate position with Takami. And she, I am sure, was convinced she would be thrown to the crocodiles for being so intimate with me. But Kamose made us feel that he wanted to understand our love and was not jealous of it. Indeed, the night that followed was more intense than anything we had shared together until then, with Takami and I taking turns to pleasure him and he us. After all, he was the king and entitled to as many wives as he wished. This way, I would keep him and enjoy myself as well. I found myself equally excited rather than jealous by this new situation. If I could see him with another woman, a woman I cared for myself, then I found that I was not jealous. As long as I could join in, that is. But for now we had to control our feelings and, as far as anyone knew, Takami was just a servant. But there was an atmosphere between the three of us now that was incredibly exciting.

The days passed. Navigation was not difficult, the river was wide enough for our boats to sail in line and the sailing itself was not complicated. I knew there were more sets of rapids ahead but we would reach our final destination before then, at an old fort that Nehsi had arranged to be repaired and supplied with a new garrison. And then we would meet our host, Takami's brother and the new king of this strange land. Although the desert was very similar to the one we had passed through for the length of our journey, it seemed somehow different as well. There was less green at the edges, fewer settlements, little evidence that anyone lived here at all. We passed some abandoned villages but no-one came to stare at us and there was no smoke visible from cooking fires. Even at night we could see nothing in the darkness of the desert. Only the brilliant sky above which seemed alive with lights. Some even moved across the sky, like the flaming arrows I had once seen when watching some of the wargames when Kamose and I were newly married. And it was totally, absolutely, silent.

When the lookouts finally announced that the fort was coming into view we were all so relieved. Shade, even more than any thoughts of food, wine, or rest, was what we craved. We had several days to rest and recover before Nehsi was due to arrive with the rest of the army, and then we would entertain King Tarka before travelling on with him to visit his own capital. It all promised to be so exciting. But as we sailed ever closer to the enormous walls of the fort, which must have been truly daunting to our enemies when it was first built by kings long in the past, there was an unease that everyone, myself included, began to feel. We expected flags, sentries blowing trumpets of recognition, signs of activity on the walls, even on the river below the walls. Signs that they were expecting us. But there was nothing, only the absolute silence. Not even the sounds of animals or birds, usually so jolly along the river, broke the stillness of the air. As we came closer we could see that the walls Nehsi had ordered to be repaired were still broken and neglected. No flags flew from the towers. The place for mooring boats was shattered and offered no safe landing. And, worst of all, of the garrison that was supposed to make the fort safe for us, there was no sign. The fort seemed entirely deserted.

Takami

I had been here before. The enormous walls, the great battlements, the imposing menace of this great intrusion into our lands, I had seen them before. Then I was much younger and was going away from my country, a gift from my father the king to the young wife of another king far away. I do not remember how I felt at the time, my emotions had changed over the years as I came to know and love the new lands I was sent to. There was so much more green, so many wonderful sights, so much beauty in the places and the people. And the friendship of the young queen that made me feel so much more like a sister than a servant. I stood beside her now as we drifted closer to the ruins of the old dock, just holding position with the gentle movement of the oars. There was tension in everyone. This was not how it was supposed to be. The king made a slight gesture with his arm and the boat moved closer to the shore. Hands reached out to tie ropes around broken wooden piles and we made the boat as secure as we could. The men had bows at the ready and swords were handed around. The other boats with us made fast in the same way. We were not many but I felt a little comfort that I was not alone.

The king was the first to step ashore, followed by his immediate bodyguard and the crew of our little vessel. The king wanted his wife and I to remain on the boat but she took my hand and we climbed onto the dock with the others. I think he realised that we would be safer together and he only smiled at her. When everyone had landed, we made our way slowly along the quayside towards the enormous entrance gates to the old fort. There were odd scenes along the way, evidence that people had been here and probably not long before. There were patches of wall which had been repaired but the materials had clearly then just been abandoned and the work left unfinished. At one point we all stopped and stared at a large patch of dark stain on the ground which could only have been dried blood. The queen gripped my hand even harder and I returned the pressure to show that I understood. As we entered into the body of the fort, the neglect was even greater and, somehow, seemed more recent. There was an area of burnt wood which looked as though a barricade of some sort had been destroyed by fire. There was even still the smell that remains for a while after a fire has burnt out. The king moved his arm again and the men spread out, to search the fort and try to find answers to this fearful sight. We were drawn to the area of the well, an obvious structure in the centre of the open area in front of the main buildings of the fort. Perhaps the promise of water drives us all when there is no other point of focus. As we approached, however, we became aware of a stench that made the first man to reach it double over and vomit into the sand. The king told the others to stay back and approached by himself, his hand protecting his nose and mouth. A glance was all that was required and he turned back, his face white. At a safe distance he was able to tell us that he had found the remains of the garrison. Their butchered bodies had been dropped into the well. We were then interrupted by one of the search party returning to us supporting the body of an old man, almost naked but for a few rags, who seemed more dead than alive. The king gave instructions that he be taken into the shade of the tall walls and water fetched from the casks on the boats. The old man started to speak but none but I could understand him. I pushed to the front and comforted him as best I could, urging him to tell me his story, to tell us what had happened here.

He gripped my arm tightly and stared around at us with wild and frightened eyes. There must have been something about us that made him relax a little, he stopped sobbing at least, but he did not release his grip on my arm. He spoke in short, broken sentences. There was much fear and much emotion in his words. His story was terrifying. Men had come to his village. Men had visited every village around, for as far as he knew. They had taken everyone away. All the men, the women, the old ones, even the children. He had been down beside the river, mending some nets, and they did not see him. He hid from them and saw the men take away his entire family. He was so afraid, he did not know what to do. Where could he go? Who could he tell? He decided to follow them, to stay hidden, to try to find out where they were going. For three days he followed, as more villages were taken and more captives added to the long lines held together by ropes. He watched as they were dragged along, as they were beaten, as some of the young women were violated, and he sobbed that he could do nothing. Then, as he was almost dead from thirst and hunger, the enormous caravan stopped at a site where many hundreds of others were being put to work. It looked like some gigantic quarry where men, women, children, everyone was set to work to dig. But they were digging what looked like an enormous ditch. An excavation deep into the earth itself. This was not a mine, they were changing the face of the land. Now he knew where they were, he had to find someone to help them. But the men driving the others to work, beating them with whips when they dared to rest, taking any of the women that they wanted, looked like his own people. They spoke his language. They were not invaders. He decided to return to his village, near the old, derelict fort. There was no point in going further on, he could only go back. When he returned, weak and delirious with exhaustion, he could not believe what he saw. There were men at the fort, men who looked different from his own people. They were singing and chanting as they built mud bricks and repaired the fallen walls. He staggered across to them and they took him in and cared for him. But he could not tell them who he was, where he had come from, what he had seen. They did not understand his words.

He must have slept but he was awoken by sounds of shouting, the clashing of swords, of men fighting. He hid himself and peered out, terrified that it was happening again. There were men in the open area inside the walls, they had come through the broken walls easily. Those that had saved him, that had been so kind to him, were gathered together in a tight bunch, their weapons thrown down, as others stood around them. Those who now controlled their fate were like the ones he had seen earlier, at the diggings. People like himself, with much darker skin. He could understand the commands that they gave, even though the prisoners could not. They identified the one who was in charge of the workers in the fort and had him dragged forwards. He looked at his captors in bewilderment. They were gesturing him to kneel, to bow before them, but he was stubborn, proud. So they slashed at his legs to force him down and then one of them, the one who demanded that he kneel, cut off his head with a single blow of an enormous sword. They laughed and they left him in the dirt. Then they gathered up the bodies of those who had refused to surrender and cut off parts of their bodies, as though these were great prizes, and they dragged the bodies to the well and threw them down. Then they tied up all of the rest and took them off. He was sure they must have taken them to the same place, to join the others they were using as slaves to dig into the land.

At this he collapsed, sobbing, and his words no longer made any sense. He was crying for his wife and his family. The king put his hand on the man's shoulder and looked around at us. His face was stern. He said that we must return to the boats, leave this place immediately. He would send an urgent message to Nehsi, that this meeting was a trap, hoping that he would not be too late. We almost ran back towards the gate, but we never made it. They had come back.

Amasis

The old man's tale, translated by the queen's young companion, chilled us all. Everyone, the king included, gripped their weapons more tightly and looked around with increasing unease. When the tale was told the decision was obvious. We could not stay here. The fort, despite its mighty walls, was not a safe place. The river was our only chance, back to the boats. If we could return to the first set of rapids, rejoin our army, we would be safe. But that was many days away and, for the moment, we were very few.

The king signalled the men to return to the boats and we helped the old man to his feet. He could not stay here, alone, and we could not leave him. So it was that the king, myself, the queen and her companion, were at the back of the group, supporting the old man, as we approached the gate. At first we could not see what was stopping the men from moving forwards, why they seemed to have bunched up at the gate. It was the king who sensed the danger even before I did, pushing the two girls and the old man through a low doorway and into the shadows beyond. His only words to them, at least all that I could hear, were 'Be still. Do nothing.' And then he marched forwards to stand at the front of his men.

They were not an impressive sight but what they lacked in soldierly discipline they more than made up for in menace, and they outnumbered us many times over. It was clear that there were many more outside even that stood blocking our way. At their head was a small man, with a face that reminded me of nothing other than a rat, smiling at what he must have thought was his cleverness. The others treated him with deference and he wore a golden headpiece, not quite a diadem or even a crown, but I thought that this could only be the man who had invited us here as his guests. This was Tarka.

He had us throw down our weapons and line up outside the gate. He walked along the line and stood, smirking, in front of the king. The king stood proudly looking down at him, he was at least a head taller, and returned his gaze without blinking. Tarka said something which we could not understand, repeated it, and then struck the king with great force across the face. All of the men made to move to defend the king and a great cry went up from them, but Tarka's men pushed us all back with spears and swords. Some of our men were badly slashed to keep them in order. The king wiped the blood from his mouth and continued to stare impassively at the little man in front of him. He said nothing. With a wave of his arm, Tarka had us moved along to the far end of the quayside, ignoring our boats, and had us all tied together in a long line, our arms secured with thick rope. When he was satisfied with what had been done, he mounted into a small wagon and had the king, his hands bound in front of him, tied to the rear. Then, with a grunt to his driver, we began to move off. We were goaded with spears and whips into moving at a fast pace, almost running, but the king was almost dragged off his feet as the wagon picked up speed. Our great adventure had suddenly become a terrifying nightmare.

Reja

I was focussed on helping the old man to his feet, helping Amasis and Takami to support him, and so was not sure what was happening at the gate. Everyone had moved off, heading back to the boats, and I expected we would join them and seek safety on the river. I was completely surprised, then, when Kamose gave me and Takami a hard push through a small, dark doorway and hissed at us to be silent. The old man was dragged between us and we ended up in a heap on the floor, surprised and dusty. Takami seemed more aware than I of what was happening, and gripped my arm as I was about to protest loudly at our treatment. Her face was frozen in fear and I sensed that there was a serious problem. All three of us, the old man not really knowing what was happening but still too frightened to do anything for himself, moved deeper into the shadows and cowered against the furthest wall. After a few moments I had to know what was happening, what danger had made my husband react as he did. There was a small window high up and I stood on some fallen blocks to peer over the edge. I could just see the men lined up outside and then saw that others held them captive with spears and swords. At one point a loud cry of anger went up from the men but it was quickly silenced. As the line of men moved off, I had to see more. I had to know what had happened to my husband. The small room we were in seemed to have another long room leading from it and, although there was very little light from only a few small windows, there was sufficient for Takami and I to run along and change our viewpoint. When we could go no further we looked again from another high window, along what seemed to be an outside wall. We could just see the long line of men, roped together and closely guarded, being marched away. I could see Amasis but, at first, I could not see Kamose. Then, next to me in the dark, Takami tensed and I could sense her pointing. At the front of the group, tied behind a small wagon and almost having to run to keep up, was my husband. And peering down from the wagon, his contemptuous face visible clearly, was his captor. She spoke only one word, spitting out a name that clearly meant so much more to her. 'Tarka.'

When we were confident that they had left and we were alone, we went back out into the light. We left the old man for a while since he clearly wished no part in any of the unfolding events. We looked around to see if anyone else had escaped but we found no-one. We did find many weapons, dropped by our men as they were captured, and decided to arm ourselves with short swords. Whether we would be able to use them or not I am not sure, but holding the weapon gave me great comfort. We looked at each other uncertain as to what we should do next. Then we remembered the old man and brought him out to join us. He pleaded for food, for more water, and we decided we would look on the boats, swinging gently at their moorings, and see what we could find that may be useful to us. There was food, water, everything, in fact, that we could need to keep us alive at least for a while, so we made a small fire, more for the comfort than for any need of warmth, and tried to think about what we should do. I had one main hope, that Nehsi was due to join us here in a few days with many men. This would give us safety, security. We could certainly stay here and wait for them. But then we wondered at Tarka's plans, clearly laid long ago, and we feared that Nehsi could have been led into a trap and his force destroyed. It was possible, that even now, he may be fighting for his life. Or worse, that we were already completely alone.

We looked at the old man, calmer now, and he looked back, sharing our fears and uncertainties. There was only one course we could take and, however reluctantly, we all knew it. We had to follow them. We had to try to rescue them. We had no idea of how, we just knew we had to try. The old man would guide us. Just in case, because we had to have some hope, we decided to leave a message in case Nehsi did make it to the fort. He would have no idea of what had happened here, or what had become of us or of the men who should be here defending its walls. I looked around for something to write on and something to write with. A message scrawled in the sand or scratched on a wall could so easily be lost. I returned to the boats and found what I was looking for in what had been Amasis's cabin. I showed Takami how to write the name 'Nehsi' and set her to scratch it in large letters onto one of the walls just inside the gate. Anyone arriving from our army would recognise the name. Meanwhile, I wrote an account of what we had seen, what had happened as far as we knew to those who first occupied the fort, and what we as the only survivors planned to do next. This letter I put into a space behind one of the large bricks I prized out of the wall with my sword, and I scratched a large ring around the brick to indicate where the message could be found. We were calmer now, probably because we had at least some sort of plan, and so Takami and I held hands for a moment before picking up our packs. We had food, water, a guide, and the advantage that no-one would be expecting us. I said a short prayer to the gods that I had always trusted. I could only hope that they heard me.

PART 4

Teti

It was just a family visit, an old man wanting to see his grandchild and those dearest to him before travel became too difficult for him. That was all anyone needed to know. Nefret and Kashta were delighted at the opportunity to see Amaja and Yrsa and the children, and they needed little persuasion to make the voyage. The river was slow and the winds were fresh, so the journey was swift. I let it be known, casually, when we were settled, that I missed my friends and colleagues from when I had been vizier and, as I had hoped, many of them came to call, to wish me well, and to share news and gossip. And so the story began to unfold.

I knew of the visit to the southern king, this Tarka, of course, and I was aware of the wargames and the main reason for them, so that the king would be travelling with a large army to ensure his safety. I was vague about some of the other details but did not think too much of the problems. The king would have thought through the many possible outcomes, and he was well advised. Nehsi was with him and I had the utmost confidence in his judgement. As long as his orders were not countermanded. But I was told that the new vizier had been concerned recently for the security of the far-flung borders, which surprised my old friends because they knew of no such problems, but they could do nothing to oppose the orders that now came forth from the vizier himself. They had heard that the army was being recalled from the south, orders had already been sent, and the men were to be dispersed to the far north and away to the distant western deserts. The very protection that the king depended upon was being taken away from him. And he was probably completely unaware of it. There was anxiety in the eyes of those that spoke to me. Something was wrong but they were powerless to put it right. They had suggested sending messages directly to the king, informing him of the changes in the domestic situation and urging him home as quickly as possible, but had been refused, even threatened for opposing the vizier's instructions. And so they did nothing. But now they felt they had a champion and they urged me to speak to the vizier of their concerns. He could not refuse to see me if I asked him for an audience, I still had considerable influence with the king, but I knew he could keep me waiting for many weeks if he so chose. He would not risk insulting me, but he could make his lack of respect clear in other ways.

I decided I would ask to see him, that I had to do, but I could also work in other ways. I still had agents that were loyal to me and many of them were adventurous men who enjoyed the dangers of the unknown. One of these, a man originally from the far south who used the name of Sheka, was asked, through mutual friends, to meet me the next day at the chapel to the memory of my old friend and predecessor. This was a quiet place across the river where we would not be overheard. It was an obvious visit for me to make, the old vizier had been my wife's father and a man very much loved and respected. Keeping a careful eye, in case there was any sign that someone was keeping a watch over me, we went as a family and crossed the river in the early part of the following day, in the cooler part of the morning when the river was still quiet. The walk up through the fields to the edge of the desert, where many such chapels were located, was pleasant and the children were asking questions about the life of the man we were here to remember. I was happy to talk about him, and the others all had something to add of their memories of him and his beautiful wife. The air was still, and the only other person I could see when we arrived was a man sitting outside the doors of the chapel wrapped in an enormous but shabby cloak, his head completely covered in a large hood. We assumed him to be the keeper of the chapel and bowed as we passed to show our respect for the office he performed. He nodded but still his head was completely covered. The children went off with their mothers to seek a shady spot while Kashta, Nefret and I laid offerings of flowers, wine and food at the foot of the statues of Kashta's parents. It was a beautiful place and I left them for a moment to their own thoughts. I felt rather than saw him come up behind me and it was only a slight surprise when he said, from very close, 'Excellency, what do you wish of me?' It was Sheka.

From a distance, even to my family, we could have been discussing the upkeep of the chapel. In reality, I was asking him to travel far to the south, at great personal risk, and to be my eyes and ears for the safety of the king. He was to find out what was happening, warn the king, if at all possible, of the dangers he was facing from his new vizier, and urge him to return as quickly as he could. He would need to use his own judgement over much of what to do and he would be in great danger if he was caught before he could reach the king. While our backs were turned, and still none could see, I gave him my ring with its seal of office, which might make it easier for him to gain access to the king, and enough gold to help him pay his way. It was a measure of the man that he accepted the mission without question, merely nodded at his instructions, and was then gone as though he had never been there at all. I felt great comfort after he had gone, that no man can think his life a failure if he commanded the loyalty of men such as this.

We spent the day in idle chatter around the chapel, looking at the many panels which told of the old vizier's life, and then made our way slowly back across the river in time for a late meal. There was a message waiting for me at the house. I had an appointment to see the vizier the following morning. Now, perhaps, I would find out what was happening. Or what he wanted me to believe was happening.

Kamose

When we finally stopped, more to rest the horses than for any other reason, I was utterly exhausted. My feet were torn and bleeding from the rough desert path and my arms ached from constantly being pulled by the wagon to which I was tied. The heat was unbearable and the thirst was greater than anything I could ever have imagined. Only pride kept me from collapsing to the ground. We had separated from the rest of my men, Amasis included, some time before, they had taken a different trail but to where I had no idea, and now it was just Tarka and a small bodyguard that remained to mock me. I was surprised that he addressed me, and also his men, in a dialect of the southern parts of my own lands, clearly useful to him when dealing with the border tribes, and I understood enough to feel quite sick inside. Somehow, not understanding your captors gives a certain distance from them and their threats. Now I had no such luxury.

'See how this mighty king bleeds. See how his royal flesh cracks in the sun. I will raise more of his skin with my whip when we reach my palace and then we will see how a king weeps with pain.'

His men laughed at this and the sense of cruelty was clearly ingrained in them all. I only thanked the gods that I had saved Reja and Takami from being his prisoners, but it did not comfort me that I had no idea at all of what had happened to them or what would become of them. After taking time to enjoy drinking from large pots of water, with nothing being offered to me, we prepared to move on. Tarka must have been reading my thoughts.

'If you try to end your suffering by throwing yourself at my men hoping they will kill you, be warned. They have been instructed to cut pieces off you but not to kill you. You will die how and when I choose, not as you would wish'.

The wagon jerked forward and I almost stumbled to my knees. I determined that I would not be dragged behind the wagon, even if I had to run on my bleeding feet. I would not give him the satisfaction of seeing my pain.

It was almost dark when we approached a high wall which stretched away on all sides as far as I could see. There were burning torches which seemed to mark a gateway and we were greeted with loud but slightly unmusical trumpet blasts as we approached. I assumed we were at Tarka's palace and I said a silent prayer that I may finally be allowed to rest. There was much fawning over the king and wild cheering as he addressed the crowd, this time in words I could not understand. Then I was untied from the wagon and dragged away into the darkness. There were long passageways, mostly almost in darkness, and we descended several lengths of stairs until I was pushed, very roughly, into a room. I could see no details, and the only sound was of a door slamming behind me and a bolt sliding into place. Then, all was silent and I was alone. I sank to my knees, trying desperately to think of something other than my pain and my thirst, and I genuinely believe I would have cried if my pride had not held me together. I had never felt so alone or so scared in my life.

Nehsi

I had tried to reason with our three guides. I made it clear to them that I saw through their plan to lose us in the desert and that I would leave them staked out in the sand to die if they did not tell us what orders they had been given. But they would say nothing. We were not where we were meant to be, that was certain, but we were not completely lost. The river was the most reliable tool for navigation in this entire land and I knew in which direction it must lie. So I knew how to get back home. But where exactly in the path to the river were we, and how close to our original destination? The king expected me to be close by to protect him and, even now, may not be fully aware of the treason being unveiled around him. I had to reach the fort and I had to move quickly. I would get nothing from these three so I had their throats cut as they knelt before me. It was a more merciful end than they deserved.

Giving orders to the column, now short of water and supplies for men and horses, we turned in the direction I knew the river to be. The position of the sun was our surest guide. I sent scouts on ahead, spreading out to gain as much information as possible, and told my officers to keep a slow but steady pace. We would stop to eat at nightfall and would then continue in the coolness of the night to make the going easier. The sand was firm, even stony, and the wagons and the chariots made good progress. We could leave some of the heavier material behind if we needed to but, for the moment, we did not know what we could spare and what was going to be essential.

As the scouts returned to give their reports I found that we all shared a common misconception of the area. We were used to a river that made its way, essentially straight, all the way from the southern rapids north to the great marshes. There was no sign of this river as far as they had been able to see. One man, more familiar than the others with this part of the desert, suggested that we were in the middle of an enormous loop in the river, so that it could have been at its nearest to the north, south or east of us at that time. We knew we had not crossed the river so it could not be to our west, but in every other way we were now effectively lost. To keep going east, risking running out of the limited supply of water we were carrying, would be a tragic miscalculation if it turned out that the river in fact lay only a short distance to the north or south. I could not move the army until I knew more. We would have to make a camp where we were and rely on the scouts to find us a way home. I was desperately afraid that, just when the king may need me the most, I was unable to reach him. It is bad enough for a general not to have an army when he needs one. How much worse to have an army but to have no idea of where to take it when it is needed.

Teti

On the day appointed for our meeting, the vizier Ramose kept me waiting no longer than the time it would have taken him to be sure he looked as noble and dignified as possible. The great doors were opened to me by servants I did not recognise but who bowed as low as my status required. I still had some respect here, clearly. Ramose rose to his feet, with a smile of welcome and his arms outspread:

'Teti, welcome. It has been a long time. Retirement suits you, you look well and relaxed. Come, sit with me, take some refreshments and talk of old times.'

I must confess his welcome quite took me by surprise. He seemed sincere, even pleased to see me. There was none of the suspicious behaviour I had been expecting. I returned his greeting and we walked together out onto the wide terrace, a view I remembered so well, and sat before a low table laden with wines and sweet cakes.

We sparred for a moment, exchanging general pleasantries and each seeking information about the family of the other, and he expressed disappointment that I had not brought either or indeed both of my beautiful wives with me. I told him of my reason for being here, of my wish to see my grand daughter and the rest of the family before travel became too trying for me, and that mutual friends and colleagues had asked me to call on him in case the troubles they had heard about with our distant borders meant that my long experiences with these areas could be useful to him. Although seeming to be casual in my offer, I had been watching him most carefully, and the sharp narrowing of his eyes at the suggestion that all was not well with the kingdom made me suspicious. An honest man, faced with serious problems that he had not met with before, might be more open to advice from one who knew so much more.

'Problems? No, there are no problems with the borders. The king is visiting our neighbour to the south, King Tarka, and has sent messages that all is going very well, and the wargames that were planned have been very successful. The army will make its way slowly back up the chain of oases to the west once the king is safely on his way home.'

The smile was casual, the tone almost conversational. It would have been so easy to believe him if I did not know from my own very trusted agents that he was lying. He frowned for a moment before continuing.

'Who has been spreading such rumours that all is not well with the borders? Such misinformation could be treasonous. It is no-one's place to question the king's actions or the dispersement of his armies. Have you discussed these matters with anyone else?'

The tone had changed, and the cosy familiarity of before had been replaced with a distinct chill of menace. He had clearly not finished trying to intimidate me:

'I don't need to remind you, I am sure, that spreading rumours about the security of our lands is treason. And those who take part in acts which are treasonous will be met with the full force of the law. The law which I represent in is totality, in the absence of the king.'

I had the impression that the last part was added more as an afterthought but the implication was very real.

'Under the circumstances, I feel I must ask you to be my guest for a while as I investigate how far the danger to the king has spread and whether you are, as I now suspect, plotting against him.'

With a wave of his hand two armed men appeared from behind long curtains, which made me realise that this whole episode had been carefully staged, and I was pulled to my feet and marched away. Even as I tried to speak, to voice my protest at this treatment, he had risen and left the room by another door. I had walked right into his trap. He could say anything he wished about what had happened to me. I could disappear without any trace and no-one would ever know the truth. Whatever plot was underway here, the life of the king was clearly in great danger and I was only glad I had already sent Sheka on his mission. I knew that Kashta and Nefret would be concerned when I did not return, but they would be powerless to act and could only accept whatever lies Ramose told them. As the door of the room to which I had been taken was firmly bolted behind me, I suddenly felt very unsafe and very unsure about my future.

Reja

We set off bravely but I knew we had so little chance of achieving anything. We did not know for sure where Tarka had taken his prisoners, or even whether he would spare them or my husband. What were his plans? And why was he doing this at all? What could he possibly hope to achieve? We had certainly been fooled so far. I could hardly believe how easily he had separated the king from his army and made him a prisoner. Was he to be held to ransom? The old man seemed less frightened now that we were moving again, perhaps he felt that we were going to rescue his family. He seemed unable or unwilling to see how powerless we were. But he knew the ways across the desert and he was all we had.

To begin with, we were able to follow the tracks left by the feet of many men and horses, and the wheels of Tarka's wagons. We had to run to make up time, we did not know how far ahead of us they were, but we also had to be careful that we did not come across them suddenly and risk capture. By the end of the day, as darkness descended around us, we had to stop. We were hungry, tired, and desperately thirsty. We dare not light a fire, which would risk giving away our position, so the night would be cold. We looked all around to see if there were signs of other fires in the distance, Tarka would not be afraid to show his position, but we could see nothing. The old man huddled under a blanket and was soon snoring, while Takami and I lay together for mutual warmth. We tried to sleep but neither of us, for some reason, felt quite so tired anymore. So much had happened, so much that we did not understand. So much had changed. We could not even think of questions to ask each other, to try to make some sense of it all. We just lay in each other's arms and took comfort from each other. It would be light soon enough and then we would have to keep on with our quest.

We found them later the next day or, at least, those they had left behind. It is always surprising that, although the skies seem empty, there are birds that can find death even in the loneliest places. It was the birds that led us. The tracks were many and confusing, and it seemed that this may have marked a parting of the ways. Many feet had taken a route away across the desert while fewer feet and the wagons had continued ahead. Why these few had been chosen to die we had no idea but the butchered remains of three of our people lay in the sand. The old man refused to look, he had seen so much suffering he had no space for more. He went and sat at some distance from the sad sight and turned his back. He was not without sympathy, he just had no more grieving left to give. I tried to see if I could recognise any of the poor souls who had met such a fate in this savage place, I was particularly anxious in case one of them should be Amasis, but I could not. They had been tortured most brutally and then beheaded. Takami retched quietly, as much at the stench as at the clear evidence of her brother's savagery. There was no point in trying to cover them, the birds and the jackals would find them just the same. I said a prayer for them and we moved a distance away to decide which of the two paths we should follow.

Very close beside the track of a wagon was a set of footprints, sometimes clear, sometimes blurred as though the individual had stumbled, but always following close as though the two were tied together. This had to be Kamose. This was the trail I wanted to follow, straight ahead and deeper into the desert. But the old man felt sure he knew where the other tracks were leading, and he was sure that the main group of prisoners were being driven to the same workings where his own family and villagers had been taken. Takami agreed that we had to know what was happening with the mysterious diggings if we were to make sense of anything at all. They were not far now, the old man assured us. So, after a longing look in the direction where I knew my beloved husband must be, suffering torments I could not imagine, I reluctantly followed the other two towards the direction where the sun sets, and where all of us will eventually go before we are reborn.

Amasis

I think we were all a little dazed by how quickly we had been taken. Whatever Tarka's plan was, it had been swiftly and cunningly carried out. The men were beaten into lines, tied with ropes, and then whipped into almost running after the wagons. And I could do nothing to help my king. The sneering face of Tarka will remain with me forever, and I prayed to the gods to let me deal vengeance upon it. It was hard to estimate how far we had travelled or even in which direction. We were given no water and no rest. Even when we stopped for the sake of the horses we were made to remain standing, the sun almost directly above us. I could feel my lips cracking and my tongue seemed to be several times larger than my mouth. Darkness brought some relief from the heat but only replaced it with a very cold night. We were bundled together to make sure we could not escape but at least it meant we had some mutual warmth as well. The smallest amount of water was passed around but so little for each of us that I think it actually made the thirst even worse. No fires were lit and only the guards ate. Tarka remained apart from the others, and they were certainly a savage-looking lot, but I could not see the king. I was afraid that Tarka had something particularly unpleasant in mind for him but I could not think why. Surely we had come as allies, trading partners with much to be gained from mutual cooperation? What could Tarka hope to gain? Capturing the king did not give him rule over our country. And he could not invade to the north while Huya had the army in place. I could make no sense of it.

Later the following day we seemed to reach a point where our paths were to diverge. The wagons stopped and the guards came together as though discussing what to do next. Tarka gave orders and we were separated from the wagons and pushed to one side, as though we were meant to take a different path, and for the first time I could see the king. He was tied to the lead wagon, as he had been from the beginning, and he was swaying unsteadily on his feet. His skin was burned by the sun and his lips were black. He was filthy with the dust from the road but I could not see if he had been beaten. At the same moment, one of the men further along the line seemed to see the king as well, and a murmur rose from those on either side of him. The man made as though to move towards the king and even pushed back the guard who tried to stop him. What followed was brutal beyond belief or reason. Clearly to make an example of him, and to cower the rest of us, the poor wretch and those to each side of him were cut free from their bonds and dragged before Tarka. Looking at them coldly, Tarka drew his enormous curved sword and, with a single, savage sweep, cut off the head of the first dissenter. Then, with a nod that effectively gave the other two to his men, he watched as they were first disembowelled alive, castrated, and then beheaded in turn. The three bodies were then further abused by having parts cut from them and stamped into the dirt. Without further comment we were then dragged on our way, with plentiful use of whips, while Tarka, his wagons, a small bodyguard, and the king, stumbling on behind, continued on the path we had originally been taking. I prayed to the gods not to desert him, and if they had any time left, not to desert us either.

Kashta

When he did not return later in the day we were, at first, not too concerned. There could be any number of reasons, he could have been asked to stay for a banquet or to attend other meetings. But we thought it strange that he had not let us know. With darkness we became more worried and as the night gave way to day we were desperate for news. Nefret and I decided that we must first go to the old palace, to seek an audience with the new vizier and ask what had happened to our dear husband. The building was so familiar, it had been my home for so much of my life, but it had also changed. There were no familiar faces, even among those who seemed closest to the vizier. As though all of the old ministers and secretaries, even the old servants, had been replaced. It had a cold air. I wondered how much, if any, of this had been the king's doing and then I wondered if the king even knew. I felt uncomfortable while we waited for the vizier to send for us and I realised that, if he did not wish to see us, we could be kept waiting for many days, until we decided to leave. And then we could be blamed for discourtesy if he should choose to call us. I tried to settle but could not. There was furniture in the room that I had known since I was a child but now it seemed awkward to sit. Nefret urged me to be calm, to wait until we knew more, but I paced the room like a caged animal. The sun was high in the sky when the door opened and the new vizier himself stood in the doorway. He smiled and seemed genuinely pleased to see us, but he had no comforting words for us.

'Your dear husband was here yesterday, a polite social call, but he left after we exchanged gossip and had some refreshments. He did not tell me where he was going. I regret I cannot help you further. Forgive me, I am on my way to another meeting. I'm sure you will find he is visiting other friends. He may even be waiting for you at your house when you return.'

With this he bowed again and was gone. There was no time to ask any questions, the door was firmly closed behind him and two guards stood in front of it. They did not look friendly. Nefret and I stared at each other and I could see that she was close to tears. She had been so sure that the vizier would have known where Teti had gone, now she felt completely lost. I held her hand for a moment and then we decided that, perhaps the vizier had been right, and Teti would already be at home wondering where we had gone.

We almost ran back to the house we were sharing with Amaja and Yrsa but they knew nothing more. Teti had not returned and there was no word of him. I knew that there were many in the city that counted themselves fortunate to have been thought of as a friend to the old vizier, and Nefret and I decided we must seek some of them out. They may have seen him or may have heard from him. Any news would be better than knowing as little as we did. Leaving Amaja and Yrsa to care for the children, trying not to worry them further, Nefret and I set out to try to find out what had happened to our husband. Some of those we sought were away on business, some expressed surprise that Teti had not visited them but were concerned for us, one seemed uneasy when he learned that Teti had last been seen visiting the new vizier but he would not say why he was concerned. We were warned to be careful with our questions by another but, again, he would say no more. We were now becoming increasingly desperate.

We had returned to the house and were pacing the floor anxiously but without plan or purpose. If the vizier was telling the truth, perhaps Teti had fallen or even been attacked and robbed on his way home. Perhaps he was, even now, lying injured somewhere, confused and uncertain. This seemed the least likely of all of the possible explanations but the alternative, that the vizier had deliberately lied to us, was the most unpalatable. What could possibly be his motive? It was young Akila who heard it first, asking her mother what the strange noise was from the door to the street. It was a light tapping, as though someone was afraid that too much noise might draw unwanted attention from listeners nearby. One of the servants made to open the door but we urged caution. There was too much uncertainty at the moment, even normal behaviour could be dangerous, but we did not know why we felt this way. The door was opened and almost immediately a man pushed his way through and helped to close the door behind himself. I recognised him immediately as one of my husband's former secretaries. He was shaking and almost crying with fear.

'Ladies, please forgive me but I had to see you. I have heard you are seeking your husband and have no news of him. I saw him yesterday as he came to the palace. We exchanged greetings and he promised to see me again before he left. There seemed to be something he wanted to ask me. I waited for him, at the gate, the only way he would leave the palace once his business was concluded, but he did not come. I waited for many hours but still he did not come. I was very worried but there were few I could ask. Everything at the palace has changed with the new vizier. People are in fear of him. Any who disagree with him are removed from office. Those that threaten his security in any way simply disappear. I tried to ask casually about the visitor, the old vizier, but I was told not to interfere. Ladies, I am very much afraid that he may be a prisoner in the palace, in the old store rooms deep inside the building. The new vizier has held others there before. Some have been released after learning their lesson, some have never been seen again. I knew that no one would tell you of this, from fear of punishment, but I could not let you worry, not knowing. I don't know how I can help you, but I had to tell you.'

I comforted him with our deepest thanks and offered him wine and a place to rest. He was clearly very much afraid. But he did not want to stay, partly from fears for our security and mostly, I think, from his own. He opened the door a little, peered out through the crack to make sure there was no one watching, bowed again briefly, and was gone into the night.

Nefret and I looked at each other, afraid of what we had learned but determined not to be intimidated. There was probably no one alive who knew the palace better than I did. I had explored every part of it as a child and had spent so much of my life within its walls. We would go to the palace, now while we would be hidden by the cloak of darkness, and we would enter unobserved and find our husband. What we would do then I had absolutely no idea, but we would not just sit here and cry about it. That was not who we were.

Reja

It was Takami who saw it first. Far away, just a slightly paler area on the dirty yellow-brown of the desert sand. My eyes were almost blinded by the intense light but she didn't seem to have the same problem. We stopped for a moment, uncertain, but then moved towards the object, cautiously. We were on a slight ridge, sand stretching away on all sides, but there were harder rocks ahead, the area becoming more rugged, now more hills than plains. When I could see what she was pointing to I thought it perhaps a bundle of rags, an animal maybe. Something not alive, anyway. But as we approached closer it moved, and what seemed like an arm detached itself from the mass as though trying to push the body up from the ground. One of us, I am not sure which, gave a slight scream and we ran towards what could only be a man trying desperately to get to his knees. He was dressed in filthy rags, hardly to be called clothes, though they may once have deserved that name. His skin was burned and blistered by the sun, a filthy matted beard obscured his features. He seemed to sense we were there but could not imagine we meant him no harm. He put up his hands to protect his head and sank back to the ground. With one of us on each side, the old man was still far behind, we tried to support him and shade him a little from the sun. I tried to put some of our precious water onto his lips, to help him to drink, but he seemed unable to swallow. He thrashed from side to side, his arms not seeming to do what he was telling them. He could not open his eyes. As I stared at him, sure there was something familiar that I knew from the past, it hit me suddenly and with a great shock. Of course I knew this face, although it had looked very different the last time I had seen him. It was Amasis.

It was not possible to give him the help he needed while we were on the ridge, in the full glare of the sun. But there were rocks ahead and there were shadows as the sun was moving around to its resting place for the night. He was heavy but, with the old man's help, we managed to drag him more than lift him and reached a place where it became quite suddenly much cooler. I tore off a large part of my already short dress to soak with water and wiped this across his face and mouth. We poured some water between his parched lips and he coughed but swallowed gratefully. I whispered his name into his ear, told him who we were and that he was safe but I do not know if he understood. He seemed to swing between an almost unconscious sleep and then sudden wakefulness, as though completely exhausted but desperately trying to regain his senses. We did not have much water left but we agreed he should have more. I divided what we could spare between wetting his burnt skin with my damp skirt and moistening his lips. He gripped my arm, tried to speak, but then collapsed into a deep sleep. The three of us looked at each other but, for the moment, there was nothing we could do but stay with him, try to keep him cool, and wait for him to wake again. Only then might we discover what had happened since we were last together.

It was another cold night but, because we were more sheltered by what was almost a shallow cave, we decided to risk making a small fire. It created some small comfort but little warmth, but the cold seemed to revive Amasis and he began to breathe more gently in his deep sleep. As we shared some of the remaining food and water, Takami asked the old man what he knew of this place and he spoke for a while, looking into the far distance. She translated as he spoke.

'These are the hills at the edge of the great desert, they stretch away further than any man has ever travelled. There are tales told of great mysteries, lost cities, armies that have disappeared into the sands. And strange people who ride long-legged animals that never need to drink. And caves that descend so far into the earth that a man may visit the gods if he has courage enough to keep going down.'

He had been here before, he said, as a young man, and that is why he knew where his family and the people from his village had been taken. And that is where this man must have escaped from. It was another day's walk, further into the cauldron of the desert heat. We asked if there was any water here, any small relief for the desert animals. We knew there were animals, we had heard them in the night. There was water, he told us, but it was not good water. It tasted like putting a piece of bronze in your mouth and sucking on it. But it could keep a man alive. Tomorrow, we would try to find it.

I was sunk into my thoughts over the tales he had told us and could not say how much time had passed. I may even have slept. The others certainly did, the old man snoring, Takami breathing gently in my arms. But I was awakened by movement from Amasis and when I freed myself from Takami's embrace I could see he was awake and trying to make sense of his surroundings. I took his hand and whispered his name. At the sound of my voice he tried to bring his eyes to see me more clearly in the faint light of the dawn and, perhaps finally recognising me, gripped my hand and tried to speak. No words would come, his throat was still raw from thirst. He tried to smile but his lips only seemed to crack and bleed some more. He winced with the pain but was clearly relieved that he was with friends. I put my arm around his shoulders, tried to moisten his lips a little, and he slept again. It would soon be light. Then we would try to find the water that might just keep us alive. I was so glad that we had taken this path. If we had not found him, Amasis would surely have died, alone in this place that even the gods had forsaken. I could only pray that, wherever my dear husband was, he might have someone to care for him.

Nefret

We had some difficulty in finding our way into the palace, the way was not quite as Kashta had remembered it. Perhaps the river was at a different height but the entrance she was seeking, down at the water's edge, eluded us. We could not risk lighting the lamp we had with us, there may be eyes watching from the high walls, but there was just enough light from the lanterns in the sky for us to make out the ground around us. Just as were about to give up, our worry and frustration mounting, and try to find another way, she gave a small cry and pulled me after her into a narrow gap almost covered by tall rushes growing from the water around our feet. We were in. Once inside, where the darkness was complete, we lit our small lamp. I laughed aloud when I saw her face, clearly now in the lamplight, for at some point she had obviously wiped her eyes but had not realised that her hands had been covered in mud. She now had a mask of mud across her face which made her look like a bandit. I hugged her and we allowed the tension to pass, just for a moment. The way ahead was narrow and we had to bend low to avoid the uneven roof of the tunnel, but we were now inside the palace and deep below the levels where most of the audience rooms were located. We were probably closer to Teti at this point that anywhere else, hoping of course that he was still where we had been told he would be.

We quickly lost any sense of time, the tunnel was long and branched several times. Kashta comforted me that she was now confident of where we were and that we would soon enter a larger passageway which served the enormous storerooms that lay beneath the palace. She had played here as a child, she whispered to me, with her then young friend and later husband, Senwasre. She paused at this sudden memory, of someone she had never forgotten but had not thought of for some time, and I squeezed her hand to share the memory. This was the time when our lives first came together as well, and we found a love for each other that had never faded. The moment passed and we continued to make our way forwards by the light of our small lamp. As we approached the end of the tunnel we could see light ahead and blew out our own small lamp so that we should not be seen by anyone guarding the passageway. We peered carefully around the corner of the wall but there was no one to be seen. A single lamp guttered in a recess on the wall some way ahead but the passageway itself was deserted. It was very quiet. Holding hands for support we made our way slowly along the now much wider and higher passage, peering into dark doorways as we went. There were other lamps lit in various recesses, most almost exhausted of their supply of oil, and we picked up one to help us find our way. The fear we had was that the room in which Teti was imprisoned may be guarded and we did not want to announce our presence and be discovered. But there was no one around and the silence was complete. Only one of the doors ahead of us was closed and our lamp showed it to be bolted top and bottom with long bronze pins. We looked at each other for a moment and then pulled back both bolts as quietly as we could. The door opened and there was a small amount of light from another lamp inside. Curled up beneath the lamp, on a simple bed of straw covered by a cloak, lay a sleeping man. But, when we approached more closely with our lamp raised to see more clearly, only disappointment. It was not our husband.

Amasis

I really was not sure whether I was still alive or was, even now, approaching the great hall of judgement. My head ached as though the embalmers had been at work on it, and my mouth felt as though it had been stuffed with an old blanket. I did not know which piece of misery to focus on first, but I prayed that I was alive because I could not bear the thought that I may feel like this for eternity. There was a sound, which I think may have been me groaning, and then I felt my shoulders being supported and a damp cloth being wiped across my face. I believe that my eyes were open but I could not see anything clearly. There was a small amount of light, I could make that out, and some warmth as though from a fire. Everything else was darkness. But the hand that wiped my face was soft and gentle, and I had senses enough to realise that my head was not resting on the hard unyielding chest of a warrior. And then I heard my name. A soft voice that I knew so well and thought never to hear again. I found the hand and squeezed it to tell her I knew she was there. And then I must have slept again.

The water that was placed between my lips had a bitter taste but it was so much better than nothing at all. I coughed but then signalled for more. As I became more alert I realised there was more light but that we must be in a room or at least out of the harsh sunlight. Gentle hands again comforted me and I was able to look around and try to understand the new sensations that I felt. There was an old man in rags, looking at me from a squatting position with the light behind him. He looked familiar but I could not place him. Then I saw Reja and, beside her, her beautiful young friend Takami. I looked further around but there was no one else. They propped me against the wall, told me I was safe, that we were in a cave in the hills, and gently asked me what I could remember of the past weeks. I closed my eyes and tried to remember what came before the pain that I felt now.

When we separated from the king and Tarka we were marched and dragged for what must have been several days until, suddenly, we came to the top of a ridge where the land seemed to drop away. There was an enormous valley beneath us but it was not like a normal desert valley, this one seemed to be full of people and noise and dust and an endless sound of hammering and digging. It was like nothing I had ever seen before. The clouds of dust almost obscured the detail and gave the whole scene a dreadful quality as though we had entered the regions where the gods sent those they wished to be punished, those whose hearts had failed the final judgement. There was a steep path and we were pushed on to descend into the chaos below. For just a few precious moments we were allowed to rest, there was even a small amount of water, while our guards discussed where we were to be sent to work. Our bonds were cut and we were dragged to our feet, some being taken one way and myself and those that remained dragged another. A pick was put into my hands and I was pushed towards a wall of solid rock and told to dig. I had no idea what I was digging for but I could see those around me being struck with whips if they paused too long in their endless labours. So I struck the rock with my pick while another wretched shape, it seemed small like a child, scurried around my feet picking up the loose material into a basket. The same was happening all around me. There were more people digging and carrying away stone than I could possibly imagine in such a desolate and desperate place. And what we were all doing it for I had absolutely no idea.

This was my world for day after day. I had no idea of how many days. We were allowed to rest for a while at the hottest part of the day, where the heat in the confined valley made the earth around us shimmer such that we could not see far ahead on either side, and there was a little mercy as the valley walls shaded one side or another as the sun travelled across the sky. For me it came towards the end of the day. We were given some filthy water to drink and something to eat that may once have been alive but had died a terrible death, rotting somewhere out in the desert. There was even talk that what we were eating was the remains of those that had died from their labours. It did not seem to be out of the question, nothing in this place operated by the normal rules. I tried to see if I could recognise any of the others around me, any that had been captured with me, but all were so covered in sweat and dirt that faces did not even look like men at all. And there were women digging as well, and children collecting up the baskets of broken stone. All wore a blank and dazed expression, as though they had parted company with their souls, gone to seek a better place than this. It was like nothing that could be described or imagined, and nothing that could be believed.

Reja and Takami listened in amazement, wide-eyed with disbelief. Not at my story but that such things could really be true, that people could do such things to each other. Takami translated some of what I said to the old man and she told me his family and those from his village would have been there somewhere in that terrible place. I often had to pause to drink but my voice seemed to be re-turning and the heat of my skin seemed to be less. My lips still hurt and I was very hungry, but I felt that I was alive which was relief in itself. When I finished my story they asked me the obvious question, how had I managed to escape and to be where they had found me.

In truth, I could remember little of what happened after I decided that I had to try to escape. Death would be certain if I did not. No man could endure this for long. There seemed to be just one part of the day when I might be successful, and I knew I had to take my chance as soon as I could before further weakness made any escape impossible. I feared almost certain capture or a lingering death in the desert, but at least I could die trying to live. At the hottest part of the day, when the sun seemed directly on top of us and the valley floor shimmered with the burning heat, the guards retreated to some tents they had erected and left us, for a while, without being watched. Perhaps they felt that there was no risk of anyone escaping because there was simply nowhere to escape to. When the time was right, I tried to keep low and moved along the edge of the valley, past eyes dulled with lack of curiosity, until I came to the same path that we had descended those days, how many I did not know, before. I made my way up the path and across the top of the ridge, always keeping low, and just ran as fast as I could. I did not know which way to run, I could not work out where the sun was at that time, and my mind was not giving me any clear advice. I just kept running. And, in truth, I remember nothing until waking up with Reja giving me water and speaking my name.

I then asked the girls how they had come to be there, just when I most needed help, and what they knew of the events that had taken place since we had last been together. As I regained more of my strength and we shared what knowledge we had, we began to see that there was only one way forward. We had to get help, both to free these people and to rescue the king, and the only way that this might be possible was to get back to the fort where all of this had started. If Nehsi had reached the fort, had found the message Reja had left for him, and had started to look for us, we might find them in the desert, but finding them somewhere was our only hope. We needed an army and that was the only one we could hope for. Reja though, had other plans. She could not go off again in the opposite direction to her husband and she was determined to try to find him. Takami would go as well, she knew this land and she spoke the language of its people. Meanwhile, the old man would guide me back to the river and we would try to find our army. It was not a good plan, but I knew better than to argue. Reja was my queen, after all, but more she was a good and loyal friend who was desperately fearful for the man she loved. I urged them both to be careful, only to watch and gather information, and to wait for the help I promised, somehow, would arrive for them. We would wait for the cool of the night and then we would go our different ways. I prayed that I would not let her down and that we would not be apart for long.

Nehsi

Finally, I knew where we were and where we had to go. The scouts had returned and the way back to the river was easier and closer than I had feared. We were above the level of the fort but we would soon be able to make our way alongside the great river, following its flow, and our horses would not have to be destroyed for lack of water. We left the wagons and the chariots for a while until we had refreshed ourselves sufficiently, and then men were sent back for them with clear directions to follow to meet us at our destination. I despaired that so much time had passed and could only worry about what had happened to the king and his small escort while we had been lured away. If they were safe within the fort, guarded by its garrison, all would be well. I had ordered supplies and men to be there to greet him, while the walls, long neglected, should have been repaired. But, somehow, I was uneasy that all was so well. We had been caught up in some plan of Tarka's and I was not sure what lay ahead. I urged the men on and sent more groups of scouts forward. I had to know what to expect and I needed to know quickly. The news they brought back to me was not good.

Of the men of the garrison, the supplies, the repairs and, worst of all, the king and his small bodyguard, there was no sign. We found what was left of some of the garrison, the stench only now abating as the well had been cleared and its filthy waters drained away. It would be some time before anyone could drink from there. We covered what we could of the men out in the desert sands and tried to honour their names. My heart was filled with thoughts of revenge but I was more frightened for the king than I had ever felt for myself. I was in charge of his army and I had let him down. I had not been there when he needed me and I would never forgive myself, however this ended.

It was one of my officers who noticed the name carved onto the wall. My name, and a great ring around a loose stone in the space below. He removed the stone and brought some loose pieces of material to me. They were covered in the neat writing of the queen. The story she told filled me with horror. The massacre of most the garrison, the king taken captive, the men with him enslaved. She, her companion, and an old man, a witness to what had happened here, were planning to follow the tracks left behind as the men were taken away and see what they could discover of their fate. Such tracks were by now, of course, long since obliterated by the desert winds and I had no other clue of where she may have gone. Deeper into the desert, almost certainly, but why go through the desert and not follow the river? I had no idea, but the boats the king and his party had used were still tied to the dock outside. I needed information, a local guide, someone who knew this desolate land. But I had no one.

After pacing the derelict walls of the fort, pretending to examine the defences but really trying to find space to think without the questioning stares of my officers, I decided that we had to complete multiple tasks at the same time. We had to fortify the base that we had, finish repairing the worst of the damaged walls, resupply with food and water, not such a problem with the river so close, we had to increase our numbers, and we had to learn more about the lands around us. And then we could go and find the king. I divided the men into teams. Some were sent to fish and gather water to fill the cisterns that once provided water for the baths. Since we could not use the wells this was our only way to actually store water. Some of the men would form scouting parties to learn what they could within a few days travel of the fort, penetrating ever deeper into the desert. Some would stand guard to protect the others against a surprise attack. I would travel back down the river to the great rapids and bring back with me the rest of the army. I dared not send anyone else, there had been so many tricks I felt that only my presence would tell Huya the seriousness of the situation. The boats tied up at the shore beside the fort did not look to have been damaged. I would take one of those. I did not want to leave the men but I had able officers and, for the moment at least, everyone had work to do. I would take only a small bodyguard to crew the boat and we would leave at once.

It would take far less time to travel with the flow of the river and I did not think I would need to be gone for very long. A few days, perhaps a week at most. We would not worry to transport the boat down the rapids, a difficult task even with more men, we would just march across the land at that point to reach the camp where Huya should still be conducting his training. He would be worried not to have heard anything for so long and I was afraid that the men would have become bored with having so little real work to occupy them. Supplies would be running low as well and I hoped that Huya would have sent some of the larger ships back to resupply. There should still be more than enough men available to bring back with me and then we would find this Tarka, wherever he was hiding, and crush him like the scorpion he had shown himself to be. At last I was feeling that a course of action was underway that may prove positive. I hated to be frustrated by inaction and by lack of a plan to work to. Now I felt I had one.

We made good progress down the river, the men proved that they could turn their hands to almost any task even though they were not boatmen by training, and within just a couple of days we came to the point above the great area of rapids where I had last waved off Amasis and the king. I knew we were close now. I wondered if we would hear the sounds of the army or even be able to smell the camps. We almost ran across the sands to the summit of the small ridge that separated us from the vast plain below. At the top we stopped in amazement and utter bewilderment. Where I expected to see tents and campfires, together with the wagons and chariots of the thousands of men that made up the army I had so recently left behind, there was absolutely nothing. The great plain, though scarred with the marks of camps, feet, horses, campfires and chariots, was now completely empty.

PART 5

Huya

I had not expected the orders but I had no choice but to obey. They came under the seal of the vizier himself. The borders far to the north and deep into the western desert were under threat, he said, and the army had to move to defend them with the utmost speed. Supplies would be sent to us on our route and we were not to delay. I gave the instructions to my senior officers to dismantle our camps and we prepared for our long march. The message from the vizier repeated his confidence that the king had sufficient body-guard for the ceremonial duties ahead and that everything was proceeding well with the royal visit. With a heavy heart I gave one last look behind at the ridge where I had last seen my friend and commander Nehsi depart with his guides, and pointed my men north into the desert. The great ships that had brought the king and his party to this place were to remain here to enable them all to return to the capital in due course. The crews were not needed here, they could accompany the army. Amasis would have men enough with him to make the journey safely down the river.

We had a long march ahead of us, via the great chain of water bodies and wells that marked the western edge of our lands and the start of the great desert beyond. We could not travel too far each day but I tried to send small groups ahead to scout the route and to try to make an advance party in case they were needed to support the border patrols. I needed to know more about the dangers we faced and the exact locations where we would be most needed. I tried not to think about those we had left behind, the royal party we were supposed to protect, and could only hope that the vizier was correct and that all was going well for them.

Once we were fully involved in our journey I had to admit I was happy to be active again. The men had been in danger of becoming restless once the initial wargames had ended and it became clear to all that we were just finding excuses for them to march, parade and stage mock battles. They had performed well in all of the tasks we had set them and I was genuinely pleased that the training had been so successful. And these were the second-level regiments, not even as good as those that had accompanied Nehsi to be the king's main escort. I was proud of our men and secretly relished the possibility that we could soon prove ourselves in true battle. I felt guilty at not being able to return home, of course, and I certainly missed my family, but this is what I loved most.

The days passed, we marched, we camped, we marched again. We found that some supply dumps had been left for us, as we had been told, and everything seemed to be going to plan. The men were enthusiastic to be going to where they felt they were needed, and spirits were high. As the distances between water depots became greater, however, and food was becoming less fresh and more and more rationed, we began to feel uneasy. Scouts had returned from far and wide to claim that no enemies had been sighted, local tribespeople knew nothing of unrest, no border patrols were found that needed our support. And then, at our furthest point into the desert, just when we were at our lowest reserves of food and water, and where we had expected to meet the enemy threatening our lands, there was nothing. I was unsure of what orders to give. This was not what I had been expecting.

I could not keep the men and the animals marching endlessly into the desert with diminishing food and water. I ordered them to make camp. I sent out foraging parties to hunt and to look for water, I sent out more patrols to search further and further into the desert to seek answers to our strange situation, and I prepared a message to be sent back to the capital to seek further instructions from the vizier. Perhaps the situation had changed and he had been unable to contact me with new orders. I had almost completed this task and was about to send for men to carry it when one of the distant patrols came hurrying back into camp. They had found two men wandering, almost dead, in the desert, claiming to be looking for me with an urgent message. At last, I thought, I had been right and the vizier had sent new orders. But the two men that appeared, dressed in rags and almost dead from the heat and exhaustion, did not look like messengers from the vizier. Indeed, they both looked far too old to have undertaken such a journey. They sank to the floor, gratefully received water they so desperately needed, and looked around as though trying to identify where they were. But one of them, despite his grizzled beard and sunken eyes, I recognised immediately. He tried to smile at me through his fatigue and gripped my arm as he tried to rise. I could hear him, a mere whisper: 'At last, at last, my dear boy. I prayed we would find you.' It was Teti, my father.

Teti

When I was taken by the guards deep into the cellars of the old palace, I was angry and confused. How dare he treat me like this. But it was pointless to try to resist the guards, it would be undignified and would certainly end badly for me. They were the vizier's men , they did not even know who I was. I knew where they had taken me but I was concerned that at least one of the old store rooms under the palace seemed to have been turned into a prison. There were no prisons in the royal palace in my time. The old king would never have tolerated it and the new king, young Kamose, would never treat anyone like this without a most compelling reason. The vizier clearly feared that either there was something I knew, or there was something I would do with knowledge I may yet acquire. The heavy door closed behind me and I was left in the darkness. But the darkness was not total, there was a small lamp burning in a recess on the far wall, but my eyes were not yet adjusted to it. And I suddenly realised that I was not alone.

The voice that welcomed me was hesitant and emotional. It was a cultured voice. He asked who I was and was I a prisoner like himself. I answered that I had been locked up here against my will and

I gave my name. There was a sudden sharp breath.

'Excellency,' the voice said, 'it is I, Nebamun, who served you for so many years. I prayed that I could speak with you again but never, never, like this.'

I remembered my old secretary well, we had known each other for many, many years, and I urged him to come forward so that I could see him and greet him properly. He appeared before me, more a shadow than a real person, and we embraced as old friends. I asked him to tell me why he was here and how long he had been a prisoner. He was clearly weak from his experiences and it seemed easier for us both to sit down on the floor. It is difficult to stand in almost total darkness and I feared he would collapse if I held him longer. He spoke with a weak voice that I could hardly hear:

'Time has no meaning here, I do not know how long I have been in this place. Shortly after the vizier came to power he removed most of the old staff, those that had served you faithfully for so long. I was away with many duties in the great temples, perhaps he just forgot about me. But when I returned, I noticed strange things, visits from people that had no appointments, that gave no identification. I tried to keep hidden as I went about my duties, hoping he would not notice me. But I heard things that made me very concerned for the king's safety. When I heard that his majesty had gone south, to visit a king called Tarka, it suddenly became clear. This was a name I had heard whispered around the palace. The men I had seen were his agents. They were not preparing for the king's visit, as it had been told to me, they were preparing a plot against him. And the vizier was at its heart. I could not go to the king, I had no proof, and the vizier would know I was working against him. There was no one loyal to the king that I could go to. I wanted to talk with you but you were far away. And then I found some papers, they should have been destroyed but they had been missed. They were translations of messages from Tarka to the vizier promising him wealth beyond his dreams, and power to run the entire country for Tarka, almost as a king, if he gave the help he had requested. Tarka also said something about a plan for taking away the power of the river which was underway if he should not get his wishes, and that our lands would no longer exist if we defied the will of Tarka. I could not understand this but now I had the proof I needed. But I was discovered and put here before I could send word to the king. I have been afraid every day that it would be my last. He has killed others who have gone against him. Some have been here for a while and have then just disappeared. I cannot have much longer. Once he has what he desires most, the kingdom, there will be no safety for anyone. He will rule by fear. That is his way. And worse, I know that he has sent orders to move the main part of the army away from the southern borders, where they are able to protect the king, with a false message, sending them deep into the northern desert where they will become helpless for lack of supplies. Then the king will have only a small guard with which to take on Tarka, once he realises the treachery that surrounds him. It may already be too late.'

He was sobbing by the time he had finished his tale and I urged him to take some water. There was very little of this and I had no idea how long it would be before we were given more, but he was shaking with the emotion of his story. The water seemed to calm him. I now knew more of what was going on around me, but I almost wished I did not know so much. He sank into a sort of stupor after a while, helpless to deal with the enormity of what he knew, his only hope for salvation now a prisoner like himself. And so the days passed, or so I imagined but had no measure of time. At one point, small amounts of food and water were passed through the door to us. We were given a small amount of oil for the lamp but my requests to the guards to send a message to my family were ignored. My friend and I were totally dependent on their good will and I am sure they would have just left us to starve or die of thirst if it had been up to them.

I was determined not to lose hope and tried to examine every part of the room which was our prison in case there was any point of weakness which we could use to escape. At least it gave me something to do. But the walls were solid, there were no windows, and the only items left stored in the room were old pots long-since emptied of their contents. Nothing we could use to escape or to help us to stay alive. I found that I must have slept a lot, the endless darkness made it difficult to stay awake because there was nothing to look at except the lamp itself. It was easier just to sleep. And so it was that I was deeply asleep when hands shook me awake, and a smell filled my nose that was sweeter by far than the stale smell of unwashed bodies that I had become used to. A lamp had been brought close to me and I could make out two shapes, leaning over me, shaking me, and calling my name. I imagined I must be dreaming and told the visions to go away, not to torment me by what I could not have, but sweet lips touched mine and I realised it was not a dream. I do not know which of my beautiful wives had kissed me but I felt a greater joy than anything I had known for a long time.

How we escaped from the palace I am not sure, even now, but Kashta knew her way through the corridors and we were soon outside, breathing the fresh, clean air that blew over the river. It was still dark but not nearly as dark as inside the cell. I found that I could actually see quite well, my eyes were so well used to darkness. We made our way quietly and cautiously along the road to the house where we had been staying and were greeted rapturously by Amaja and Yrsa. They had been so worried for us all. I introduced my friend to them and he gratefully accepted food and wine. With more light now available to us I could see how thin and drawn he was. We both wanted to clean ourselves and dress in more comfortable clothes, and so some water was heated for us. Part of me wanted to relax and enjoy being free but a larger part knew all too well the danger we were in. Our escape would be noticed the first time the guards brought food. This would be reported to the vizier and he would send out parties to search the places we were most likely to have gone to. We were both far too dangerous for him to be allowed to live. And our families would be in danger in case we had told them what we knew. I urged everyone to gather together what they needed and to leave the house for somewhere safer. We made it seem to be a game so as not to frighten the children, but I am not sure they were fooled. I knew the capital well and I knew I still had friends, loyal to me and loyal to the king, especially in the great temple complex. We would find a safe place for everyone and then I would do the only thing I could do to try to bring down the vizier's plans. I could not travel south to help the king, I did not know how I could reach him or where he would be, but I knew now where the main part of the army would be and, if I could get to them, I could try to persuade them to return to the capital and restore the king's order. I had crossed the great desert once before, far to the western borders, but then I had been much younger and stronger, and I did not underestimate the difficulties or the dangers. But no one else could be trusted with such a mission or would be better able to influence the army commander, I prayed it would be Nehsi or, better still, my son Huya, to order the army back to attack the vizier. I had to go. And a measure of my friend's loyalty, Nebamun said without hesitation that he would come with me. I was not sure he would be strong enough but he was desperate to do something, anything, to restore his pride, because he lived with the idea that he had somehow failed the king. And so it was decided. We would leave immediately, still cloaked by the protection of the night. We would have to find a boat to cross the river, we could not trust a boatman who might later give away our plans so we would steal a boat and sail it ourselves. We put together what supplies we could, there would be a limit to what we could carry, but we could not take pack animals which would slow us down and leave a trail it would be easier to follow. I hoped we might find some on the way who would help us but there was more than just a chance that we would not make it at all. There were tears from Kashta and Nefret, and anxious looks from the others, but we had to go. And not look back to what we may never see again.

Amasis

He was a strange companion but he seemed to know the desert

tracks. We could not speak each other's languages but we communicated with gestures, and there eventually came, I think, an understanding between us that was almost a friendship. We had a common enemy, the desert, and a common purpose, to find the help that we needed to release the captives and to gain revenge for those no longer able to do so against an enemy that had struck us so treacherously.

I seemed to grow less fatigued with the days rather than more so, which puzzled me, but I suppose it was the difference between being free with hope and being a prisoner with none. We found small pools of stagnant water in caves, used I am sure by the animals of these parts. We saw occasional tracks, even droppings, but we saw no other living creature, not even a bird. Our food was soon gone but hunger seems less when thirst is so much more a concern. We eventually knew the river was near, long before we could see it. The ground became greener, there were birds, and the air itself tasted sweeter. When we came close we ran as though our lives depended upon it and splashed into the water, dancing like fools. We drank, we submerged ourselves to cool down, we stripped off the rags we still called clothes to try to clean them, and then we tried to find some food. There were birds but we had no weapons to catch them. There were fish but they were far too clever to swim into our open hands. We found the remains of bird nests but there were no eggs. He showed me a trick he had used before when on long hunting trips and peeled back the outer layers of some tall plants he gathered at the river's edge. The fibrous, centre part of the stem had a sweet taste which, under the circumstances, was better than the finest meal I could ever remember. The roots also were edible, he told me with gestures, but they needed to be cooked and we had no means to make a fire. But it was the first food we had eaten for several days and it gave us the confidence that we just might succeed after all.

We decided we were most likely to be upstream of the fort and would follow the edge of the river, moving downstream, until we located it. Water was no longer a concern and we knew we could not be more than a couple of days walk from our destination. At one point we came across the remains of a small but deserted settlement and searched the simple houses for anything we could eat or use. We found some stale beer, some hard bread, some dried fruit. Best of all, tied up amongst the reeds and well hidden, a small boat. It was a simple design but it floated and it would carry us onwards. Things were looking better with each day.

When finally in sight of the fort, I could see our boats still tied up against its walls and signs of smoke from fires within. Someone had occupied the fort but it was not clear at this stage whether they were friend or foe. I did not want to shout to announce our presence only to be confronted with Tarka's mercenaries, but equally I did not want to be taken for an enemy raiding party by Nehsi's men and fired upon from the walls. I did not want to arrive suddenly, surprising any on guard who may have become sleepy with idleness. I decided we must pull into the bank and approach, quietly, on foot. I needed to know who we were dealing with. I left the old man, I still did not know his name I suddenly realised, in case he was less cautious than he needed to be, and made my way quietly towards a break in the walls. It was exactly as I approached more closely to the small gap that a face appeared, of a man carrying a basket of material he was clearly about to use to repair this weakness in the fort's defences. I do not know which of us was the most surprised. Thankfully, because I had no weapon, he did not immediately attack me but called out to someone else to come quickly. And the language he used was my own. I shouted through the gap to give my name and to ask for help to enter the fort. Faces appeared, some disbelieving, but then I was clearly recognised even though I must have looked wild indeed. The welcome was ecstatic. Just when they knew so little, here was someone who had returned from the wilderness to tell them what was happening. Helpful hands made way for me and I stumbled down onto the wider walkway below. I asked for Nehsi but was told he had left to bring back the army of Huya, still in camp beyond the first set of rapids. He was expected back at any time but the deputy commander was sent for with shouts and cheers. It was so good to see friendly faces. Suddenly remembering the old man I had someone go and bring him to the fort, warning them to be careful since he would not understand their words and would be very frightened. Finally, we were safe.

I was not sure of the order in which I wanted to do things. My list was long. A wash, a change of clothes, removal of the hair from my face, a meal, some wine, to share news. In the end, we seemed to do almost all of them at once. And all of the time I was trying to explain to the officers what had happened to us from when we had been captured by Tarka and his men, what had happened to the king as far as I knew, where I and the others had been taken, and how I had escaped and only been saved from certain death by the queen and her companion. I told them of the old man and how he had witnessed the fate of the garrison, and of the terrible fate of his people and our own captives in the desert furnace. And I told them that the queen had gone with her companion, deeper into the desert to Tarka's city, to rescue the king and how we must set off to help them without delay. We could not wait for Nehsi's return. Even if we had fewer men now than we might have when Huya and his men joined us, we were losing valuable time to help the king with every day that passed. We had to leave immediately, as soon as the men and the horses could be assembled. We had an army here, albeit not a large one, and we must not waste any opportunity to strike against our enemy. Messages could be left, detailing our plans, and the others could follow. Since I was, at least technically, the most senior officer present, even though I was not a soldier, the order had to be obeyed. Luckily, the men agreed and seemed very anxious at last to be taking the fight to the enemy. We would leave at the end of the day when it was cooler and march across the desert by night. The old man would guide us. He too finally seemed to feel that we were no longer running away and that his family and his people might, at last, be revenged. I hesitated about using our boats to take at least some of us onwards, I knew that Tarka's city must be on the river but much further upstream, but I also knew there were many more sets of rapids between us and there, and there was neither the time nor the spare manpower to carry them through. We would all cross the desert. With a common goal and a common purpose. And if our king had been harmed, then we would leave nothing of Tarka's kingdom remaining behind us.

Reja

The old man had given us our directions, he had told us how the sun should be in the sky by the different parts of the day, and the lanterns in the sky at night. We had a small amount of water but there were small wells, he had told us, just about as far apart as a man could endure travelling in a day. But he had told us to avoid the day, if possible, and use only the cooler hours of the night. We would reach the river again, before too long, and could follow it to our destination. Then there would be water to drink, plants we could use to sustain us, and maybe even villages which could help us and shelter us. Tarka was not well liked in this land and people would help us, he was sure.

Our food was almost gone but we were less afraid of starving than of dying from lack of water. We waved them goodbye, Amasis and the old man, and then sat for a moment looking around us at the desolate emptiness. We had both been driven by a sense of urgency, of purpose, and we had succeeded in finding our dear friend and felt such gratitude to the gods for guiding us so well. But now we were alone, in this vastness, with a mission even more important but feeling even more helpless. How could we, two girls not warriors, tired, thirsty, hungry, and scared, travel so far, against a powerful enemy, and rescue a man who would undoubtedly be closely guarded, who may even no longer be alive. I suddenly felt overwhelmed by my emotions and the tears and the shaking would not stop. Takami held me in her arms and slowly, only slowly, her gently soothing voice calmed me down. She reminded me that we had armies somewhere in the deserts around us, we were really only going to find out what was ahead so that we could return and pass the information on to others better able to deal with it. We were not going to fight, only to look and to gather information. She knew the royal palace where Kamose would surely be held, she spoke the language, and, if we could get close enough, she would either go in alone or try to disguise me as her servant and we would explore together. I appreciated what she was trying to do and I hugged her but I was not fooled. There was a real chance that we would be discovered and the thought of either of us falling into the hands of her brother was more than I could bear. The only way to avoid this was too frightening to discuss but I think we both understood what might have to be done.

By now the day was cooler and we decided it was time to move on. We drank the last of the water that we could not carry and then set off for whatever awaited us. It was better to walk during the hours of night, there was enough light to see our way and the lanterns were our friends, guiding us ever in the right direction. There were rocky ridges as well as open plains and we kept, as far as we could, to where there might be shade once the sun had risen higher into the sky. On that first morning we took shelter where a small cave offered itself, but of a well there was no sign. But we were out of the sun and we slept soundly, wrapped in each others arms for some physical comfort. I must have had a dream, because I was with Kamose and he was breathing loudly and heavily over me. His kisses were wet and his tongue was hard. Even his breath was unpleasant. I struggled to understand this and fought to wake up, pushing him away from me. Takami was still breathing gently in my arms, but the source of my uncertain dream was watching me, sitting patiently a short distance away. He was a large dog of uncertain parentage but he had a pleasant face and looked at us with curiosity and not ferocity. I shook Takami awake and we both reached out for him. He approached with a smile, or at least that is how it seemed, and we made a fuss of him. He was obviously used to people and this made us realise he must live close by. And that meant a village and people who might help us. We let him lead us home.

We were a little surprised at how close we must have been to safety and the shelter of a small village. It was just a jumble of a few simple houses, made of mud brick and thatch, but the villagers lived from fishing and we gazed with wonder at the enormous river that we came upon quite suddenly. Our river. People came to look as the dog barked, and we were soon surrounded by the villagers, with a mix of fear and curiosity. Strangers were very rare here and often only brought trouble. But we must have looked harmless because we were quickly made welcome and given food, water, and kindness. Takami was able to tell them a little of our story and they looked with increasing wonder that we may have come from so far away. That we all lived beside the same river was incomprehensible to them but it filled me with a renewed sense of hope.

We stayed with them for the rest of the day, resting and trying to regain something of our previous selves. We were dirty, our hair was matted, and we looked like wild creatures from the desert, which is just how we felt. The city we were aiming for was only a few more days away by foot, and we accepted the offer of passage in a small boat rowed by one of the villagers which would make the journey much easier, perhaps taking just one day. He had fish to deliver to the markets and he would take us close, but we would not put him in danger by taking us to the walls themselves. We would walk the last part, choosing our time carefully after observing from a distance. The villagers gave us clothes to replace our rags, and we went down to the river to wash the filth of the desert away. To immerse myself in the cold water was almost ecstatic and we washed each other thoroughly and with increasing intimacy. It had been so long since we had been able to do this, and I think we both forgot that we could be discovered at any moment by a curious villager. But we both needed the relief that it brought. As the day ended we sat with the villagers around a communal fire and told a little of our adventures. They were curious about our land and knew nothing of the terrors that had overtaken other villages. Perhaps because the fish they caught were needed in the city nearby, they were safer from being taken to the diggings deep in the desert. But one curious incident they mentioned, which Takami had to ask about with several questions, left us puzzled. It seemed that we were not the only strangers that the villagers had seen recently. It seemed that a man had passed this way only a few days before, a man who came out of the desert as though he owned it rather than as if he had barely survived it. He had asked for nothing from them and seemed to need nothing. A man dressed in an enormous shabby cloak with a deep hood.

Nehsi

We stared with disbelief at the empty plain before us and I was both confused and a little afraid. I was afraid for my army since it was not where I expected it to be, and I was confused about who had given the orders for it to be moved. There was no way that Huya would have taken it upon himself to remove what was, essentially, the king's bodyguard unless he had been told to. There were only three people with that authority: the king, myself and the vizier. I know it had not been me, it was possible but I thought unlikely that it had been orders from the king, which meant that the vizier must have sent orders without consulting me first. This was serious. Either there was an emergency so great that the army had to be moved before its general could be consulted, and that must be serious indeed, or there was a plan to separate the king from his army that originated with the vizier. Since this was a man I had already formed a deep distrust for, this is where my thoughts travelled. But what to do about it. That was the question that faced me.

There were boats still tied up along the river, very large boats that had brought the king and his party so many weeks before. But they had no crews and were beyond our small number to take back to the capital, even though the water was running well and they would not need to be sailed. I thought of taking the risk anyway but then realised that arriving back at the capital without the army would take away the very weapon that kept me safe. I would be walking into whatever trap the vizier was laying. No, the only thing I could do was return to the fort and rejoin the part of the army I had left there. We could either go south to confront Tarka with the numbers we had, or return north to confront the vizier. I still had an army, even though it was now only half the size I had originally planned for. It very much depended on what I could discover about the fate of the king and those that had been taken along with him. With a course of action decided I was much relieved, and we quicky returned to our small boat tied above the rapids and set off back to the fort. The river was against us and it was hard work, but I had no hesitation in taking an oar myself and helping us to move forward. Now I was in a hurry and hoped that nothing else had happened that I had not predicted.

It took us a few more days to make the return journey, it was much harder moving against the flow of the river than with it, but we worked well as a team and we knew each other well. We knew each other even better by time the walls came into view at last but I never felt that I had to stand on any false dignity as their commander. We were all soldiers and we were determined to accomplish our mission, whatever the difficulties we encountered.

Once again, the situation we found when we arrived was not the one we had left behind. This was becoming far too common an experience. The fort was deserted, although the small boats were still tied up alongside the old quayside. In fact, there was another small boat with them that I had not noticed before. Someone new had been here and they had arrived from further up the river. They had certainly not been on our part of the river or we would have seen them. Suspecting that my deputy would have employed the same trick that the queen had used, I looked for a message in the hole in the wall which still bore my name. There was a paper inside which told of the return of Amasis, of the fate of the king as far as anyone knew, and of the brave action of the queen and her young friend in going after them to gather what information they could. The army, I read, had set off in pursuit and would follow a pattern of lights across the sky which would take them to Tarka. Since they had taken everything with them which could have provided us with food or anything other than water to drink, we decided to set off after them immediately. But this time, we would take one of the smaller boats and continue our way up the river. Even if we didn't go as far as Tarka's city, we could surely make up for some lost time and catch up with them eventually. If there was going to be a fight I wanted to be part of it. It was my army and I was not going to let anyone else take them into battle if I could help it. I had had quite enough of turning up late to my own war.

PART 6

Kamose

The darkness was almost complete but there was a small gap in one high corner of the wall where some light penetrated. It was not a window, it was far too small to be a way out, but I could put my eye against it and see sunlight and the sky. I felt all around my prison but it seemed to be completely empty. Empty of anything useful that is, but occasional scurrying sounds made me realise that I was not the only living thing in there. There was no real idea of time but I was grateful that my small hole in the wall told me when it was day and when it was night. And there were a lot of both.

After trying to humiliate me on the journey to his city I suspected that Tarka would have similar trials in mind for me during my captivity. I was determined not to yield but I had little idea of what he might try to do to me. I had no liking for pain but, in truth, had never really experienced much until now. I was more afraid of seeming to be weak than of anything that he may try to do to me. But, as the days passed, it was almost as though I had been forgotten. I was not starved but the nature of whatever the guards threw through the door onto the floor for me was impossible to identify. I only hoped whatever it was had died fairly recently. The taste was utterly vile. I do not know exactly what I was given to drink. I suspected that it had been foul water to begin with which the guards had added to when they wished to relieve themselves. I tried not to drink more than I absolutely had to. In desperation, I tried to keep myself busy. I exercised as I had been shown when I started some military training. I was already king and so could not go into the army, as I would have done if I had only been a prince, but I took lengthy instruction in weapons and had become quite accomplished at driving a chariot. I certainly enjoyed the wargames and secretly wished that I had been given the chance to lead my army into a real battle. So I pushed myself up from the floor, as I had been shown, achieving lifts with only one hand which pleased me greatly, and I ran as hard and as fast as I could, without moving from the same place, for as long as I could endure. I was determined that I would not come away from this as a cowering wretch, slumped motionless in a filthy corner. But, in truth, I know that exercising to exhaustion was really only to stop me from descending into the utter depths of despair and misery which is what I feared the most. Hardest of all, I tried not to think of Reja, whose beauty, whose softness and gentleness, were the most wonderful things in my life. We had been a little adventurous recently, her with Takami and then the three of us together, but it was Reja that I wanted and no one else. If we all survived this I would make sure that we were never apart again, not even for a single day. And definitely not for a single night. We would look after Takami of course, but we would not be with her in the same way again.

And so my days passed and I began to wonder if this was how my life would end. In this dark hole, drowning in the stench of my own waste and drinking the filthy waste of my guards. I wondered about family, so very far away, who would never know the truth about what had happened to me. I imagined that I would never see my mother again, or my real father. And I vowed that I would not be afraid to acknowledge Rusa as my father if I came through this. I was not ashamed of him, why should I pretend that he meant nothing to me. It insulted him and it insulted my mother. She had loved her husband, the king, that was no lie, but she also loved another. Such things can happen.

While my mind was full of such thoughts I heard the bolts sliding back on the door. Either this would be more of the slop they gave me to eat or, perhaps, they would finally be taking me to some degrading death. I stood up to face them. They would not see me cowering in the corner. Outlined against the light, the guard stood still in the doorway. He seemed unnaturally stiff. And then, slowly, he sank to his knees and, without a sound, slumped forward to the floor. He was replaced by another, a large man who seemed swathed in an enormous cloak. I could not see the face revealed when he pulled back a deep hood, but the voice was clear and confident.

'Majesty. Please follow me. We have far to go. I was sent to find you. I am called Sheka.'

Huya

The tale he told me, his voice breaking from the thirst he had endured for so long but still strong with the passion of his mission, filled me with a sick horror. The danger we faced was not from an external enemy, as I had been made to believe, but was far worse. An enemy at the heart of our government, the most powerful man after the king himself, working against us, plotting against the king and everything that was precious to us. We had been drawn away from the south, leaving the king without the protection we had planned for him, and were now being expected to wander these western deserts until we exhausted our supplies and were so weak we were no longer a threat to the vizier's plans. But thanks to the courage of my father, we would not do as we had been instructed. We would march back to the capital and restore order to our lands.

There was still much that I did not understand, pieces of the puzzle that could not find a place. What was happening in the south? Had Nehsi reached the king? Was the king really in danger or had that part of the plan failed as well? There was so much I needed to know. And should I return south, where I may be needed, or move directly on the capital where I was most certainly needed? I could split my army but then risked having insufficient forces on either front. I decided that I must first cut off the head of the serpent who caused the most risk to my king. If the vizier remained to give orders, pretending to act in the king's name, he could make changes that would make our survival impossible. Even if the king failed to return, we could safeguard his throne until a more stable succession was established. Having dealt with the vizier, I could send forces south to aid the king if that was to prove necessary. But there was also the question of what other treachery this Tarka may have planned. Perhaps even now there was a hostile army heading north to take the capital. Nehsi may have been defeated, the king and his family may be prisoners or worse. But one thing was certain, if I remained here I could accomplish nothing. I had to be in the capital and I had to move quickly. I outlined my plans to Teti and he agreed that it was most important that we first stabilised the government and rooted out the evil that had set itself in place there. Without the stability of the capital, the throne itself was at risk. I gave the orders.

The men were confused, of course, to be marching yet again, this time back home to where so many of them had started those many weeks before. It was impossible to explain so complex a plan to so many but I was anxious that they would understand what was at stake. I briefed my officers and they passed on the news that we marched to protect the king from a plot against him at the heart of government. The guards they would face at the capital would not be our own men, but mercenaries brought in by the vizier to protect a traitor. They would fight because they had much to lose, their lives would certainly be forfeit if they failed to protect the one who paid them, but their main strength lay against unarmed civilians. They would not be a worthy opposition to trained soldiers. I knew that my men would fight if they were told to fight but I wanted them to understand what they were fighting for. Such men made far better soldiers.

We did not have the supplies necessary to take so many men and animals back across the desert directly to the capital, still many days away, but we could go via one of the great desert wells and take enough water from there to complete the journey safely. It was essential that we came from the desert ready to fight and not in desperate need for rest. And it was also important that our progress was not observed, with messages sent back to the vizier allowing him to prepare his defences. If he had spies out to look for us, reporting back on our positions, we had to find them and stop them. I sent out scouts of my own with instructions to watch for watchers and to bring back any that they found. There were few wandering tribes in this part of the desert but it was possible innocent travellers might be caught up in this business. I did not wage war on innocent travellers, but they would have to prove themselves first. And then, the final part of the problem, we would have to overcome the capital's single most formidable defence, the mighty river itself. We would have to cross the river in force while trying to retain the element of surprise. This was the part I felt would be the most difficult. I had prepared many plans during my career, at the request of the king and of his father before him, for the defence of the city, putting myself in the position of attacker and devising ways to thwart myself, but I had not thought I would be the one trying to attack it for real. I knew all too well how difficult this could be.

Takami

The palace and the city around it were not as I remembered. The dirt, the poverty, the feeling of menace from the walls and the guards. This was new to me, this was not the palace I left as a child so long ago. Reja and I had been brought close to the city, as we had been promised, and had made our way from the river in the early light of the new day, when there were few around to see us. There was a market, of sorts, being set up but there seemed little to trade for and less to want. My first concern was to try to make Reja look a little more like me and a little less like herself. Her lighter skin and long straight hair made her look different from my own people and questions would certainly be asked if we were not careful. We had brought some clothes with us from the village and I dressed her in a long robe and headdress that managed to cover most of her body. Then, as carefully as I could, I rubbed a mix of burnt wood ash from the fire and mud from the river to darken the skin of her face. It was far from perfect but, with much of her head covered by a long scarf, it may avert any obvious curiosity. We picked up a couple of baskets from a stall when the owner was distracted and carried these with us to make it seem we were here with a purpose. All the while we were slowly, casually, circling the walls as I looked for any way in that might not be overlooked by the guards. The walls were not in good repair and we soon found what we were looking for. Checking carefully to see that we were not observed, I pulled aside some of the wiry scrub that had grown up where the foundations of an old gate giving access to the river had been rotted by years of dampness and neglect, and led the way through a narrow gap into an area I knew would eventually lead to the cellars and a deep well. The thumping in my chest made me feel quite unwell and my breathing was fast and shallow. Reja gripped my hand tightly and I knew from her trembling that she was as afraid as I was. But now we were inside and we had to keep going.

It was completely dark in the narrow tunnel and we fumbled to light the small lamp we had been given by the villagers. It contained only a little oil, all that they could spare, and we had a smouldering wick held in some damp leaves. Unfortunately, when we came to need it, the wick had gone cold and its fire had died. I could sense Reja's disappointment in the darkness next to me and we reached for each other, eventually making contact with our outstretched fingers. Our hands locked together and we agreed not to let go until we had a better idea of where we were. Moving slowly forwards, I tried to sweep around with my foot and my free arm to be sure I knew what may be around us. There were signs that the palace was in very poor repair these days, it had never been so in my father's day, and the floor was littered with debris fallen from the walls and roof. More than once one or other of us let out a small cry as we hit our heads on the jagged edges or roof of the tunnel. How long we had been moving I could not say but, quite suddenly it seemed, we could see light ahead of us. It was only a small patch of lesser darkness rather than the brightness of the day outside, but it gave us something to aim for. The walls of the tunnel also became a little clearer as we approached what seemed to be a flickering reed lamp held in a recess on the wall and we became more cautious. Someone put the lamp there, and it would have been to light the area ahead for a reason. These tunnels would not be wasting precious lamps if there was no one to see them.

It was the sound of running feet that alerted us, there were men somewhere ahead, many men, and they were now shouting to each other. Instructions, curses, even the metallic sounds of weapons being sheathed or unsheathed. Reja and I shrank back into the darkness and listened to see where the men may be going. I could only make out the odd word, the sounds seemed to repeat and cause confusion as they passed along the tunnel, but I heard the word 'king' used more than once. But which king? Were these the men that guarded our king, a prisoner somewhere in this awful place, or were they afraid of their own king, my brother? When the sounds seemed to have passed along, we dared to move a little closer to the lamp itself. I was leading the way and had almost reached the end of our little stretch of tunnel, when a shadow fell over the opposite wall. A man, moving quietly, was approaching, and I could see he had a weapon drawn. Perhaps I gave a slight gasp, I was not aware of it, but a hand suddenly reached around into the tunnel, grasped my arm, and I was dragged out of my hiding place into the larger space beyond. Wide-eyed with terror I put up my arms to defend myself, only to be gripped around the waist and squeezed so hard I almost screamed. A hand covered my mouth and a face right next to mine whispered my name. When my eyes could see clearly the man who held me, I almost wept with joy. It was Kamose. He must have guessed, or perhaps just hoped, that I was not alone, for he moved me around, still holding me tight as though letting me go would prove that I was just an illusion, and called for Reja. It was hugely comical to see his reaction to her mud-blackened face as she appeared from the darkness, and I believe that if he had come upon her first, without warning, he would have struck out at her as though she was an evil spirit. We all three of us hugged and sobbed and hugged some more, and despite her filthy face the two of them kissed and kissed until I thought they just might lose control. This was not the place. And then I realised we were not alone. Standing still in the shadows behind Kamose was another figure, tall and broad-shouldered, wrapped in an enormous cloak. I could not see his face in the shadow cast by a large hood but, when he pulled the hood back, I could see he was, in fact, an extremely handsome man, probably only a little older than the rest of us. As though forgetting his manners, Kamose introduced us all. Sheka was his name and I had a strange feeling that we had met before, made even more odd by the intense way that he looked at me. But there was no time for exchanging gossip. We were in a very dangerous place, the king's escape had clearly been discovered, and men were searching the palace for him. The area outside would almost certainly be searched as well. it was Sheka who directed us.

'Majesty, ladies, we cannot leave the palace while men search so carefully. They will know the king has gone but they may have no idea how long ago he made his escape. The one place they are unlikely to look for him is back in the cellars where he was a prisoner. I suggest we return there for a while, search for clean clothes for those that need them, and wait until night has fallen around us. Then we can make our escape from the palace and the city'.

I took his point about the clothes, realising for the first time that the dreadful smell was actually from the king himself, and that no disguise was now needed for Reja. We could all do with a short while to calm ourselves, wash, change and, if possible, find something to eat and drink. Once we made our way from the palace we would have a long, difficult and very dangerous journey ahead of us and we would not be able to stop to do any of these things. Although Sheka spoke the language of the king very fluently, I had the feeling that his natural tongue was closer to my own. I wanted to know how it was that I felt that I knew him. And I wanted to know him very much indeed.

Amasis

I was concerned that we may be watched, that Tarka's spies would take warning of our approach and give our enemy time to prepare for us. We had scouts away to both sides and well ahead but they reported no foreign eyes upon us. But we made dust that could give us away from a great distance and I still worried. Complete surprise would give us a great advantage, the more time they had to prepare for us the harder it would be. I had no idea of the size of the force we would face or of their quality. Of my own men I had no misgivings, every one was worth ten of any enemy, but even so we could face being seriously outnumbered. And we must not arrive for battle exhausted by our journey across the desert. The enemy had the advantage, this was their home and they had the shortest route for resupply, but we were not beginners and we knew our business.

We moved by night, it was surprisingly easy to see our way, and this kept down the dust as well. In the early hours, when the desert night was coolest, we even had water forming on the metal and the harnesses of the wagons and chariots. It took only a little practice to arrange to collect water in this way, mainly for the animals, and the men experienced less thirst themselves from breathing the cold night air. We saw animal tracks and I sent men out to hunt, away from the column. Fresh meat would be a bonus after the dried food we had endured for so long. They had some success and we all ate a little better for at least a few meals. The portions were not large between so many, but the taste made each mouthful special. I observed the men carefully as they marched and was pleased to see that they walked purposefully, they walked upright, they carried their weapons firmly, and they were not staggering as though the desert was winning. We were just moving towards a battle of our own choosing and I had every confidence that, when we arrived, we would strike fear into the hearts of our enemy. Tarka had clearly thought he could carry out these atrocities and then retreat deep into the desert to hide from us. He would be disappointed.

As the land became more rugged, there were opportunities to climb a little higher above the desert plain and see further ahead. We had camped beneath such a system of ridges, enjoying some shade from the sun almost directly above us, and several of us were taking advantage of the height to try to work out exactly where we were and where we still had to go. There was dust on the horizon, a wide cloud which seemed to hold its position in the air for some time. It could have been a storm, we had all experienced such things, but I somehow doubted it. It looked to me like the dust an army raises as it charges across the desert. If so, they were far too far away to be charging at us. They would be exhausted long before they came in sight of us. They would probably not even know we were here. But one whose eyes were sharper than mine gave us a clue. There were a small number of tiny dots ahead of a much larger group of dots, he reported. The ones in front were surely being chased by the many more behind. We looked at each other in disbelief. There were some we knew to be ahead of us, and they would certainly be chased by others if they had succeeded in making their escape. If this was the king and his wife and her companion then the gods had indeed been looking after them. Now, it was our turn to do what we could to take over. By the size of the dust cloud that was pursuing, they were many. But maybe, just maybe, we could surprise them.

Kamose

I had so many questions for my rescuer when he first spoke to me at the door of my cell but he simply put a finger to his mouth as a sign that I should wait. Then he gestured with his arm to indicate we needed to move away from here as quickly as possible. I was happy to go with him. He seemed to know the tunnels well and I followed as quietly as I could behind him. I had picked up the sword dropped by the fallen guard and felt comforted by its grip. My companion did not hesitate as he took turns in the many passageways, only dimly lit by guttering lamps. At one point, where I could see a small doorway ahead of us, he paused and looked carefully inside. It was though he remembered this place as having some use but there was nothing in his hands when he returned. For a moment our positions in the passageway were reversed and I began to lead the way. There seemed only one way to go, after all. It was then that I heard a slight sound, a gasp rather than words or actions. There was someone in the tunnel just ahead, I was almost upon it, and instinctively reached around to grasp whoever was there. I intended to pull them out so that my companion could thrust his blade into them if they resisted. But where I expected a guard hiding in ambush, I found myself holding a soft hand and felt the slender body of a woman. She had her eyes tightly closed and I could not believe that I was looking at Reja's dear friend Takami. What could she possibly be doing here? As I wondered if I may be mistaken she opened her eyes and clearly recognised me too. We embraced with a wide-eyed passion and I could not get out the words to ask if Reja was with her. I pulled Takami with me to the entrance of the passageway and called out Reja's name. There was another figure in the darkness but it was not my beloved wife. This looked like an aged crone, swathed in a long dress with a filthy headband covering a dirty, blotchy face. My disappointment was so deep it almost overcame the joy of my escape. But then the crone pulled back her scarf and I saw the long hair that had been hidden. And the smile, nothing came close to the magnificence of my wife's smile. She came to us and the three of us embraced and kissed and hugged. I could not believe how much had changed in such a short time. I almost forgot my new friend and introduced him to Reja and Takami. It was strange, but he took Takami's hand and bowed, almost as though he knew her, but then we had to move away from this place before more guards came. We had seen and heard them in the distance over the last part of our escape. My absence from the cell, and the dead guard, had clearly been discovered. It was Sheka who suggested we return to the cell where I had been held, as the least likely place the guards would search again. We needed to wait until dark before leaving the palace, we would certainly be seen if we left in daylight, and we needed to find food, water, and some clean clothes. We had all been away from water for so long it was difficult to say who had the least unpleasant odour. But I don't think it was me.

I could not bring myself to go back into the room in which I had been held, the girls looked in out of curiosity but were repelled by the smell and by the body of the guard still sprawled in the doorway. But we found another room nearby and, using our lamps cautiously, explored for anything that may be useful to us. We had to keep a careful watch, we were still in a very dangerous place and guards could return at any moment, but we felt that we had a plan and that it could offer a sound escape. We decided we would use the way that Sheka had come into the palace rather than the tunnel used by the girls. This would bring us out close to some ruined houses that would provide more cover. We needed to steal some horses, we would have to move fast and be prepared to be chased if we were spotted. We had no idea of how far we could get before we were seen but we knew it was very likely to happen at some point. We would head for the river since lack of water was our greatest fear. There was always the possibility that help may be on its way and this may be the route they would choose. I prayed that my people would not have abandoned me. I could not believe the courage shown by Reja and Takami, to come so far alone and penetrate the palace itself to find me. And who was this mysterious Sheka? He had done the same and with even more success. I owed him my life yet I knew nothing about him or how he had managed to appear just when I needed him. And what of the others, of Nehsi and Huya and Amasis? I had so many questions.

Those that had been my guards clearly had a room of their own nearby in which to sleep and eat, though it seemed every bit as much of a prison as my own cell. I supposed that at least they could go outside when they wanted. But there was some water in a large pot, some dried fruit, and best of all a couple of old shirts hanging up as though to dry. My need and Reja's were the greatest so we stripped off to wash and change while the other two talked quietly together. I had the impression that Takami felt she knew this man, or at least that she wanted to know him, and we left them to find out more about each other. Anyway, the need that Reja and I had for each other after so long meant that there was one thing we just had to do first. It happened quickly for both of us, and I had to cover her mouth with my own to keep her quiet, but it was one of the best we had ever had. Perhaps it is the nearness of danger, even of death, that makes us appreciate the true value of what we have.

Teti

When Huya gave the order to march on the capital, I felt both relief and fear. I was relieved that I had accomplished my mission, it had seemed often enough in the desert that we would not make it, but I was fearful in case it was all for nothing and the king whose throne we were trying to save was already dead. The succession was not clear, the fate of the queen equally unknown, and the vizier was the most logical man to take the throne. He could claim that it was only until stability was restored, but he would never relinquish power once he was crowned. The men were eager to be going home as well. The wargames had been successful but they had marched for many weeks and were now tired and restless. This mission had given them a renewed purpose and I knew we could depend on them. Huya had discussed his plans with his senior commanders and I had been invited to listen and comment. I knew he had made many plans for the defence of the city and that, if anyone, he was the man to understand the flaws in those plans. I was comforted when he told me that the plans he had made were in his head only, they had never been written down, and the vizier would be unacquainted with the military situation regarding the defence of the city. At least, he had no reason to believe that he would. The city had only a small garrison and the men, when he last saw them, were totally loyal to the king. If the vizier had imposed a new commander on them it might make the situation more complicated, but he was sure that if his men saw that the enemies they were told to fight were, in fact, their own comrades and their old commander, they would rally their support to the king. But we still had to surprise the vizier and that meant crossing the great river with a large number of men without being seen. And most of the boats would be on the other side if we arrived at night, the most obvious time to attack while keeping the element of surprise. But Huya had a plan, and it seemed the only plan that would work.

We would not attack the city directly. We would approach from some distance upstream, take whatever boats we could find, and drift down with the current, steering at a slight angle, and use the power of the river to take us across. We would land as many men as the boats would allow, those unable to cross by boat would continue to march to the city on the 'wrong' side of the river. Thus, we had no idea for the present of how large an army we would have for the attack when it came. Once the attack was underway, more boats could be sent over the river to bring the rest of the army to support us. If all went well, we would capture the palace and the vizier, and whatever bodyguard he had around him, before the rest of the city was aware there was anything happening. This would avoid panic and unnecessary casualties. It was a simple plan, I only hoped it was not too simple.

The days passed in disciplined movement, stopping at the hottest time to rest men and animals, and trying to keep down the choking clouds of dust. Scouts reported no eyes were observing us and that a place had been found, near one of the large temple complexes just in sight of the capital, where a number of boats had ben captured. We would arrive by nightfall and would then begin our assault. Huya asked if I would accompany the first party since my authority, upon capture of the vizier, would make a transitional government easier. It seemed that I was to be vizier again, whether I wanted the post or not.

It was a dark night, the light from the sky at this time was less than we had when we were crossing the desert, but that would help us. We could pack only a small number of our men into the boats but the ones we had were the best of the best. The others, and all of the horsemen, the chariots and wagons, would follow the river and wait for us on the opposite bank. Huya had learned his trade well and his men had fought in many different ways and in many different lands. They were used to unconventional warfare and were highly adaptable. The old king, my dear friend Senwasre, had called them 'marines' and I knew they were the best we could ever have hoped for. And so the boats moved away, the men using their hands as paddles to make the boats drift gently and silently across with the current, aiming for the far bank. We would land a little distance from the great temple, and would use the cover of the enormous buildings to approach the vizier's residence. We could only hope that he would be at home.

Kamose

I was curious about how my rescuer, and Takami as well, seemed to know this place so well. Both had found their way here unaided across a vast and empty desert, and both had found their way inside. He told me that Teti had sent him, chosen him because he knew these lands, and that my old friend was suspicious of the new vizier. Teti had not given him too many details but he had picked up for himself that all was not well. I knew then that I should have listened to Nehsi, I had brushed aside his concerns when they should have shouted a warning to me. If the vizier was, indeed, involved in this in some way, there was a real danger that he may already have moved to seize the throne or appoint his own commanders over the army. I wondered what had happened to Huya, to Nehsi, and to Amasis. They had all been left in their own way to deal with matters over which they little control. I cursed myself for accepting so innocently what this evil Tarka had let me believe. All of this was my fault and I deserved the gods to desert me. But I vowed that, if they did not desert me, I would win back their approval and their support. I would fight for my throne and for my people. As long as I drew breath, I would be their king. But I pushed him further, I wanted to know more, and he hesitated slightly, looking at Takami, before continuing.

'I grew up in this place, my father was the chief of the army for the old king, and I accompanied Princess Takami when she was sent to your court as a gift between kings. I was little more than a child myself, my father thought the adventure would be good for me.'

My surprise at this news was total, and I looked with different eyes at the beautiful girl I had taken so much for granted. I had thought her a servant, a mere companion for my wife, before matters developed further of course. But a princess! I was delighted and at the same time seriously concerned. If she was the daughter of the old king, she must also be related to the new king. She looked sad when she told her part of the story, how Tarka was her twin brother, and how she feared that he had murdered both their father and their elder brother, who had been destined for the throne. She wanted to know the truth but was afraid at the same time to have her fears confirmed. That was why she had wanted to come here, to confront him, but was now afraid that all of her fears were true. She knew that she would be killed if her identity was revealed, Tarka would want no alternative version of the lies he had told to be known. She had remembered Sheka, not much older than herself and a supportive friend during the long journey to the north, but they had not seen each other since that time and both had grown up not knowing anything of the life of the other. Now, I noticed they held hands in the darkness, and I was pleased for them both that they had found each other again. But there was no more time to exchange memories, the danger for us all was far from over. Indeed, it had hardly begun.

When Sheka judged that the time was right, we began to make our way back through the maze of passages that would lead us eventually to the outside of the palace walls. We approached each corner carefully, listening for the slightest sound, and kept only a single small lamp burning to show our way. We were all now well used to the darkness and it seemed that the walls were trying to guide us rather than hold us back. We heard no more sounds of guards and saw no other lights. As we approached the final corner, Sheka signalled with his arm to put out the lamp. Now there was the slightest lightening of the darkness ahead and I could make out a window, small but clear. I could see the sky outside, for the first time in I knew not how long. Near the window there was a door and Sheka opened it quietly. Realising his way in could have been discovered, and this may be a trap, he did not go outside immediately. We all listened but there was no sign other than distant sounds from nearby houses as though people were going about their normal business. We moved through the door, weapons held ready.

There were other houses close to the walls, small and neglected, as though long abandoned. We found our way inside one of them and made our way carefully to where there had once been a shuttered window, now gaping open to the darkness. All seemed quiet. But there were sounds, in the distance, of horses approaching. These animals are not well suited to the desert and I was surprised that there seemed to be so many around. I suspected that they would not be well treated and would be regarded by this king as expendable. A number of horsemen came into view and pulled up not far away. One among them was giving orders in a loud voice, his arms waving angrily. It was Tarka. I felt Takami next to me stiffen slightly as she recognised him. It was not clear what he was shouting about but then two men appeared at the gate dragging between them a third man, almost on his knees. I recognised him as one of my guards. I had no feeling of sympathy towards the man but I was still a little surprised that Tarka had him forced down to his knees before him and then held down with his arms grasped firmly behind his back. He was begging for mercy but none was shown. With a single blow, Tarka swung a heavy club down upon his head and he was felled like an ox. Blood and gore splattered Tarka's shirt, we could see the spray by the light of a number of large rush lamps held by the guards, and I felt Reja almost retch in the darkness beside me. Tarka showed no emotion and merely stepped over the fallen man, making his way back inside the palace. The other guards followed and, for the first time, we could see our means of escape. If we could reach the horses, we just might have a chance to get away. There was just one slight problem. The horses were guarded by an enormous man, armed with an equally enormous curved sword.

It was Takami who acted first. She said something quietly to Sheka and then, pulling the top of her dress down slightly below her shoulders, she stepped out into the darkness. She started to sing a soft tune as she walked in the direction of the horses, she clearly wanted the guard to know she was coming, and she swirled her dress around as she walked. She could even have been dancing as she sang and the overall effect was definitely provocative. She bowed lightly towards the guard but did not walk directly towards him. In fact, and now I could see her plan, she was moving around him, so as to distract him and have him turn his back to us. As soon as this was done, Sheka ran from our position and came up behind the guard with surprising lightness and deadly effect. A dagger thrust into his exposed neck and he fell without a sound. The way was clear. We were careful not to mount the horses too soon, the noise would have drawn attention, but we walked with them as quickly as we could until we reached the edge of the city. The term suggested more than there was since the whole area was poor and neglected, hardly enough houses to make a typical village in my own land, but the palace added a certain status, I suppose. But, once clear, we quickly mounted and set off, Sheka leading the way. We had no idea how far we could get before we would find ourselves pursued. We had little water, even less food, and our only weapons were a couple of swords and two small daggers. But we were free, and had the hope that comes with an end to torment. Somewhere up ahead there should be an army looking for us. I said a prayer to the gods that this was, in fact, the case, and that we would find them before it was too late.

Nehsi

We were too few to make much movement against the river and I quickly regretted my decision to keep to the water. We had no fear of dying of thirst but we just might end up being carried directly back to our starting point. I had a new respect for the men who had brought our boats so far. But we pulled as hard as we could, each of us to an oar, all differences of rank forgotten, and when we were exhausted we tied up to the bank for a while and rested. We fished, with some success, and I felt that we were at least keeping up our strength rather than wasting it. After a couple of days of this relentless punishment I decided that we had come far enough. By my estimate, the river had taken a wide loop and we must have made up for many more of the days that the others would have been marching. There was a range of hills between us and the desert beyond, and I reasoned we could see enough from the elevated ridges above to know where we next had to go. Such a large army could not travel in these sands without making clouds of dust and we should be able to see them from some distance away. That was my plan, anyway.

We secured the boat to a large boulder beside a small creek and gathered together what we could carry. It was early in the day and it would be a little cooler for the hardest part of the ascent. With good fortune, we would find a cave or at least some shelter before the hottest part of the day. The going was not easy but we made good time. The weeks of demanding desert survival had made us hardened to the conditions. I was determined to carry as much as my younger companions but by the middle part of the morning I was beginning to regret my pride. As we paused for a rest and to drink some of our water, now warm and unpleasant but better than nothing, I did not protest as two of the younger officers carefully divided my load between them. I was more than twice their age, and I felt that it was time to give my pride a welcome return. And to rest my aching back.

The top of the first ridge was welcome enough but it only revealed another ridge still to be climbed further on. We found a stretch of rock which provided some shelter from the sun overhead but there was no water so high up and no sign of any animal we could hunt. We decided to rest for a while and then continue as the day became cooler. If we could find no sign of the army, we might have to return to the boat and decide whether to continue further upstream or to return to the fort and then back to the north and home. This would be a very difficult decision to make and I hoped that it would not be necessary. After a short rest we all seemed to feel better and I felt much more confident. We set off again at a steady pace and made the top of the next, and final, ridge, by mid-afternoon. We could hear something before we could see it and the sight from the top of the highest point, like a hawk looking down from the sky on the plains below, filled me with awe. While we had been wandering among the hills two great armies had come together and a battle was raging below us, the figures like tiny insects so far away. We could hear the sounds of swords, of horses, and of men in combat, but the sounds were not in time with the action. We could not see clearly who was fighting, but by the formations as they attacked I just knew it must be my army at last in battle with Tarka. Several different areas of the battlefield were in action at the same time, and I saw for the first time what the gods must see when their subjects squabbled below them. This was the view that a general needed. I could see where a weakness opened up in the enemy's flank but that a squadron immediately peeled off to take advantage of it, breaking through and beginning an encircling manoeuvre. I could see where reserves were being moved around to relieve and attack just where they would do the most good. My army was being well commanded, I could not have done better, and I wondered which of my officers was in charge. It could not be Huya, of this I was sure, but whoever it was would be promoted if he survived. But now I had to get down there, before it was all over!

Amasis

Because we had been waiting, watching the approach of the enemy dust, our own clouds had settled. If we remained still, they would not know we were here. The heat from the sand created waves in the air and even as they closed with us they would be uncertain of what they were seeing. And because they were all riding hard, they would not see clearly anyway. And so we waited.

When it was clear that there were four riders in front, seeming to be trying to escape from many more behind, we reasoned that this could be the king, the queen and her companion. The fourth rider perhaps a rescuer or someone also escaping from Tarka. The order was given to move slowly forwards, in line abreast, in formation to give battle. We had the advantage that they would have been riding hard while we were relatively fresh. At some point we were seen and there were signs of great confusion among the pursuers. The four riders seemed to gain extra strength, perhaps our pennants were recognised, and trumpets were sounded all along the line both to welcome them and to signal attack. It was a joy beyond anything I could have imagined when we closed with the four riders and our ranks opened to allow them to pass through, and I recognised who they were. I pulled up my own horse to ride back to greet them while the rest of the line continued forward. The king and I embraced, the two girls dismounted and almost collapsed onto the sand with exhaustion, and the fourth man, dressed in an enormous cloak, simply wheeled his horse around and rode straight back to join the attack. The king also had no time for words but waved a chariot forward and climbed aboard with its open-mouthed driver. All I heard as he rode off was the command to take him to the front of his army. I called for others to assist the queen and then did the only thing I could. I rode off after them.

The dust created by so many charging and swirling men made it difficult to see but I could hear sounds of combat all around me. The enemy were a very mixed lot. There were some horses, but not nearly as many as we had, there were small wagons but no match for our chariots, and many men on foot, exhausted from already running for so long. There was much confusion among them, with most seeming to fight as individuals rather than as an army. It seemed typical of a mercenary rabble, undisciplined and used mainly to terrorising civilians. Small groups were being cut down by our men and they seemed to lack any strategy for either defence or attack. I decided that I would have to find the king, somewhere ahead in the dust, and be sure that others protected his back. With this sort of fighting it was easy to forget that enemies were all around you, not just in front. Something I had once learned myself, the hard way.

Kamose

There is water in this desolate place, if you know where to find it. And our guide certainly knew the desert. We tried not to ride too hard, the horses were our only realistic way of making it through the desert if we were pursued, and we wanted to look after them. We found a shallow well in a hidden valley and took advantage of the small amount of cool water and the shade. There was even a small amount of thin scrub vegetation which the horses chewed eagerly. Someone had dug this well and it made me realise that people actually lived here, in this awful place, and called it home. We had never seen any sign of them and I wondered what life they had that they valued this place. The valley went nowhere, however, and we soon had to resume our way across the merciless burning sand. I know that Sheka was concerned at the tracks we were leaving behind us but there was nothing we could do about this so he just kept looking back to see if he could see any signs of pursuit. We were sure it would happen, just not when.

The darkness of that first full day was a blessing for the coolness it brought with it. We finished the last of our food, had nothing to offer the poor horses, and settled for what little sleep we could get. Sheka and I divided the night between us, to watch from a high pillar of rock, to see if there were any signs of pursuit. It was unlikely that anyone would chase us in the darkness but it was always possible. As it happened, all was quiet. I heard sounds in the night, there were animals scavenging around somewhere, and for a while the horses were restless, but the night passed and we went on our way. It was about the middle of the next morning when we saw the dust behind us.

The horses were superb, perhaps they responded to the kindness we had tried to show them, and they gave everything to help us. The going was soft in places but firm in others, and we made what speed we could. It was not possible to guess if they were closing on us but we could not outrun them for long, that I knew. We could run until the horses dropped and then stand and fight, but I knew we would have little or no chance at all if we found none to help us. I tried not to think of the end. I knew I would not let that animal take Reja alive, but would it be a cowardly end to take my own life as well? It was Sheka who drew me back to the present by signalling that there were others ahead of us, lying in wait. He shouted to keep going. They may be friends rather than enemies that had managed to encircle us, but I could make nothing out through the trembling air. Trusting to the gods, we rode on.

I strained my eyes ahead, trying to make sense of the vague shapes I could see beginning to form before me. I could see gold shining in the brilliant light, I could see chariots, and I could see pennants flying. This was an army and a very disciplined one. I heard trumpets and I could see they were moving forwards. Then, there were cheers and cries I could understand. These were my own people, the army that I had prayed had not deserted me. Our horses almost seemed to sense that help was close by and gave a renewed surge of energy which carried us into the body of the army which opened to let us through and then closed protectively around us. I had no idea if our numbers were equal to those of our enemy but I had no doubt in my mind that we could beat them. I could hardly stop my horse before leaping from it, recognising the face of my dear uncle who grabbed me and swung me round with joy. I begged him to look after the ladies while I shouted for a chariot riding close by to pick me up. I think I shouted to the driver to take me to the battle and then we were gone, swallowed up in the dust. This was my fight and I would be at the front of my army when we met Tarka. He was mine.

Teti

The quiet murmuring of the river was the only sound. I could sense the other boats around me but they were completely silent and I could hardly even make out their shapes in the darkness. At the front of our boat, Huya was keeping watch for the bank which we knew must be close ahead. We struck some reeds and the boat was immediately slowed. Hands pulled us to the shore and ropes were attached to fire darkened bronze spikes which were driven silently into the mud. Without any signal being necessary, the men piled out onto the bank, bows at the ready, and took up positions, prepared for either defence or attack. We gave a moment for the others to join us and then moved forward, no commands being spoken. Although the sky was dark, we had the faint lanterns to guide us, we could see the walls of the great temple ahead of us, darker against the night sky. There were a few flaming torches along the walls but I could see no sign of any guards. It was too early even for the priests to be going abut their sacred business. All was silent.

We had decided to keep to the outer walls of the temple and to make our way directly to the palace where the vizier was most likely to be in residence. We had no idea if he would be guarded, but we hoped that either his guards would not offer resistance when they saw who we were or would not be our own people. I did not want to kill our own people, doing their duty but not knowing or understanding quite who they were serving. The main gates to the palace were guarded, as we knew they would be, and two men stood idly chatting beneath a number of bright torches. They were not keeping a good watch, I could see Huya shake his head at their laxness, and they were taken completely by surprise by the men who came up behind them. They were not the stuff of heroes, and threw down their weapons with looks of surprise and terror. The mighty doors yielded to only sight pressure, they should have been secured from within with yet more guards, but now the way was clear. Fearing an ambush, as always when an attack goes so well, Huya waited for all of his men to reach him before moving forward. We had sent boats back across the river for reinforcements before moving on the palace but it would be several hours before they would all reach us. We needed to move more quickly.

The inside of the palace was well known to many of us, and we were almost able to run through its passageways to the quarters I had once called home. Nothing seemed to have changed since I was last here. We paused at corners, looking around carefully in case of guards who could raise an alarm, but we saw no one. It struck me as a little strange that we did not even see servants going about their duties as the day started, it was certainly becoming lighter where we passed the enormous windows that looked down on the river, but the palace was quiet. By now I was sensing that all was not as we had planned, that something was wrong, and my worst fears seemed to be confirmed when we arrived outside the doors to the vizier's private quarters. There should have been guards here but, again, all was quiet and deserted. Huya and I looked at each other before pushing open the great doors. There was no one at home.

Nehsi

I finally reached the valley below, covered in dust and sand, my clothes in disarray and thoroughly exhausted, but, at last, I was back with my army. As soon as I was spotted a cheer went up and a horse and weapons were brought for me. I asked who was commanding the army in its attack on the enemy. The man holding my horse while I adjusted the reins looked at me with surprise, telling me, as though obvious, that it was the king. At last, I knew he was safe. But then, with a shock, realised of course that he was far from safe, and set off at a gallop to find him. To lose the king now, after so much had passed and after I had begun to despair of ever seeing him again, that would be unforgivable.

The dust was choking and I rode past small groups of men fighting, some wounded, some dead, from both sides, and signs that the enemy was demoralised and close to collapse. But the fighting was not over and would not end until their leader was dead or captured. I had to find this man Tarka. Further cheers went up as I was recognised and arms waived me in the direction where the fighting was still intense. By now I had gathered a large number of men around me and we rode together to where a large cloud of dust showed where the battle was still raging. When I came closer I could see that, like some dream which had been disturbed before it had ended, all action seemed to have stopped, as though time itself had stopped, and that men were gathered around two chariots which seemed to have collided and locked together, their horses standing dazed at the remains of their traces. The men had formed a ring around two figures, one standing, his sword by his side, and the other kneeling as though begging for mercy. I dismounted and ran forward, the others making way for me in silence. Now it was over.

Kamose

I wondered, at one point, if every battle was like this. I felt strangely detached. I could see men fighting, I could hear the sounds of swords clashing, of men screaming, of horses straining at their harnesses and choking on the dust. But I could also see where there were gaps in the fighting, places where men were fighting well and places where help was needed, and it came almost without thinking to wave men forwards to attack or sideways to fill gaps, and they went without hesitation. Men cheered as we passed, my driver handling his horses with an expertise I could only admire, and we seemed to float across the field of battle like gods ourselves. There were arrows in the air, I could even sense that some had passed close by, one even hit the frame of the chariot close to my leg, but none of it seemed to affect the inner me. I was above it all. I had never felt such exhilaration, such power. Now, for the first time, I understood why men went to war. There was no feeling like it. And I loved it!

Then, in the distance, as though he was uncertain whether to stay or to run, I saw him. I recognised his face even through the dust and the dirt, and I felt a hatred I would never have believed possible. I dragged the drivers arm in the direction of his chariot, speech was impossible in the noise, and we closed with him at great speed. He saw us and tried to get his own horses to turn, but the animals were clearly terrified and were not obeying his commands. He may have hoped to turn them away from us but only succeeded in making them run as fast as they could towards us. He was not charging, his fear was obvious, but we closed at speed and I knew we would collide. My driver was no beginner to combat and I almost closed my eyes when, at the last moment, he moved the horses slightly to the side so that the chariots collided but the horses did not. We were all thrown through the air, the wooden frames crashing and splintering behind us, the horses screaming, but we landed in the sand and I rolled over, my head spinning. I do not know if my ears had been affected by the crash but I was not aware of there being any sound. Everything was played out as though in a dream. I could see my driver lying still on the ground, I was not sure until later that he had survived the crash, and men were moving towards us. The fighting seemed to have stopped, at least for a moment, as if those involved had witnessed something that would decide its outcome once and for all.

I was the first to stand and picked up my sword from where it had fallen into the sand. Tarka was still alive, he had blood on his face but was still aware of what was happening. He looked around with scared eyes at the circle of men forming around him, my men, and he tried to rise to his feet. I gestured with my sword that he was to remain on his knees. I had never killed another man before but I knew that this scorpion had no right to live any longer. My only thought was whether I should grant him a merciful death and kill him now, or have him taken as a prisoner to be executed before the people he had terrorised and abused. I was aware of another standing close behind me and turned to see Nehsi. I almost did not recognise him he was so filthy with dust and his face covered in unkempt hair. Then, realising that I must have looked every bit as frightful, I smiled and we embraced. I waved towards our prisoner and had him dragged away to be kept in chains until I decided what was to be done with him. There would be no mercy, of that I was sure, but he had hurt others, not just me, and they deserved to know why.

Huya

Somehow, Teti and I just knew that we were too late. The palace was too quiet, the lack of guards and servants too unusual. The empty room just confirmed it. But where had he gone, and when had he left? We secured the palace, mounted our own guards, and roused what staff remained. Many were familiar faces and greeted Teti as though a spirit had returned among them. A most welcome spirit. They bowed before him, kissed his hand, and cried with relief that the old days were returned. They spoke of the horrors they had witnessed with the new vizier, of staff beaten for the most minor mistakes, of people, even senior ministers, terrified at his summons. The kingdom had been ravaged by his guards, mercenaries from other lands who cared for nothing but gold. And they had been paid well. He had talked openly about the death of the king, about awaiting only proof of this before taking the throne himself. There were witnesses to his greed and his crimes, his treason against the king, and he would be punished with the utmost severity, if he could be found.

We had decided that we would make the capital our base once the rest of the army had crossed the river to join us, and would send scouts to find out what we could about what was happening. We knew so little. Was the king safe? If not, what about the queen, Nehsi, and the rest of the army that had gone with him into the desert? Were the borders secure or was an invading army even now heading towards us? We had to know. And we had to find the vizier. He could do less harm now that we controlled the capital and the army, even if he had bodyguards of his own, but he had to be found. I was discussing the arrangements with Teti for him taking over the role of vizier again, even if just for a while, and we had sent word for our families to join us, when there was a commotion in the passageway outside. The door was opened and my deputy asked for permission to interrupt us. He had found something, he told us, that we might find of interest. It had been hiding on a boat moored at the royal quay, as though about to make its way onto the river at first light. With a signal to someone behind him, a body was thrown through the doorway to land, in a snivelling heap on the floor before us. It was Ramose, the vizier we had been looking for. Or at least, the former vizier.

PART 7

Takami

He did not recognise me at first. But when I addressed him as 'brother' he stared wide-eyed. He knew why I was here, to find answers, and he knew I would see through his lies. He had killed our father, I knew this, and our brother as well, but I wanted him to admit it. He was far from an intimidating figure. He had always been less than he had wanted to be. In height, in looks, in dignity. He was no king. he was just a little man. I hated him when he used to torture me and even small animals when we were children, and I hated him now. He had tried to brand me with a hot iron one day when he had caught me watching him, but I had run away from him and told our father. The king had beaten him and he had truly hated me ever since. That is one of the reasons my father had sent me away, and I had been so happy to leave the palace, my home, and travel to make another home in a distant land. But I would revenge my father and my brother. And I would try to make it right with my people. They were good people and they had been wronged.

I stood with Sheka as my brother was brought before us. Tarka looked at each of us in turn, wondering what his fate would be and who would decide it. He trembled, I could see his eyes desperately trying to seek a way out. Kamose came to join us and we looked at the snivelling wretch who had caused so much suffering to so many. And then Sheka asked a question that made me understand why he had come so far to help us. He wanted to know if Tarka had killed his father as well. At this point it seemed to become clear to Tarka, perhaps for the first time, that he was going to die. Perhaps he thought Kamose would show him some mercy, not wanting to execute a man who was bound and helpless, but now he knew. It had been decided. The king gave him a simple choice. Tell Sheka and I the answers to the questions he had been asked, admit to the deaths of so many of those we had loved, and his throat would be cut and he would die a merciful death, however undeserving. But if he continued to lie, he would be impaled and his skin peeled off while he still lived. This would be a most agonising death that would last for as long as the executioner could make it. I took little pleasure in seeing him squirm and vomit, even as the thought of the end that awaited him made him lose control of his bowels, but he finally admitted that he had had them all killed because they stood in his way to the throne. Even Sheka's father could have raised the army against him and had to die. He seemed, for a moment, almost defiant, as though these killings could be excused for his ambition, for his destiny. But we had heard enough and a nod from the king was all that it took. I felt a certain sadness that he had been spared a longer death but, at least, I knew he would find no place among the gods. The king ordered his heart to be cut out and burned and for the body to be left out for the hyenas to scavenge. At least we could leave something for those that made this place their home.

What was left of Tarka's army offered no resistance once their paymaster was dead. They had no personal loyalty to him. The king offered them mercy if they would serve their new king and queen instead and they all, without hesitation, sang praises and assured him that they would. But I don't think the king trusted them any more than I did. They would be sent on missions where their survival would be unlikely. He was not sparing their lives, merely postponing their deaths. But it struck me that he had said 'their new king and queen' and I looked at him for more information. He was in conversation with Sheka and the two of them looked back at me and nodded. Both held out their arms for me to join them and I looked at Reja for support. She took my hand and we both moved forward. The king had a plan and Sheka had agreed. It now just depended upon my approval. Since I was the old king's daughter, I had every right to rule my father's kingdom. But I would be stronger if I ruled with a man beside me. And who better than Sheka? He asked if I would accept him as my husband and together we would rule this land that had been abused for so long. I was very happy to accept.

Kamose

It was Amasis who reminded me that our work was not yet finished. The old man who had guided him had watched the battle from afar, afraid and not understanding what was happening, but he had now come down from the high ridge where he had sheltered to remind us that there were still those that needed our help. As I was discovering, there was more to any battle than just the fighting. We had wounded to care for, exhausted men and animals who needed food and water, shattered vehicles to repair. We had some enemy wounded as well, but they would not be a priority. And there was time, finally, to reunite with old friends, Amasis and Nehsi, and exchange our stories. Takami and Sheka had asked for an escort to help them to return home and to start rebuilding their people's confidence and I asked for volunteers. There were many who felt that the challenges and rewards of a new life, in a new place, would be worth the hardships and I wished them all well. We would be partners and allies, they were not going as a conquering army, and we would try to meet again before too many summers had passed. Reja and Takami embraced, with many tears, and promises that they would look back on the times they had shared with great affection. A look also passed between myself and Takami, but it was a look which spoke of brief but happy memories shared and of goodbye. She was someone else's now, and I would never come between them.

The remnants of Tarka's army I sent into the desert to find food and I was not interested in how many came back. Many would desert, others would squabble among themselves. They knew enough not to risk reforming to fight us, we were too many and they were far too few. And anyway, I let it be known that no mercy would be shown to any who promised loyalty and then abused our trust. If any came back at all, they would have proved themselves and could join us. But now we had an army to return home and many desperate people to rescue. There were even some of our own in need of help, if they still lived in that dreadful place that Tarka had created in the desert. I also wanted to know the purpose of the place that Amasis had described, but I knew the one person who could have told me was no longer able to do so. I sent the old man with enough supplies and enough men and waggons to accomplish his mission. The rest of us would make our way back to the fort where the survivors could eventually be cared for. We would make it ready for them. We would then have to find our boats, return through the rapids to where the bigger ships had been left and then, eventually, make our way home. And what would we find there? What had become of Huya, and did the vizier still hold any power? I would deal with him harshly when I found him. I had no great fear that he would oppose me, not with the army returning to confront him. Even if he seized the throne in my absence the people would not support him over their legitimate king. He would have told them that I was dead, the only way he could have seized power. They would see that he lied and they would turn against him.

And now I felt more like a king than I ever had before. I had led men in battle, faced death, and I had been sincerely praised by my generals. I had defeated the enemies of my people, and I had restored the cosmic order that was the purpose of any king. I felt that my father, and the king who had ruled before me, would approve. I only prayed that I had done enough to satisfy the gods as well.

Reja

It had been rather more than the adventure I had imagined when we first left from the capital those many months before. But as we returned, after a restful journey down our beautiful river, the memories of the danger, the hardships, and the fear slowly subsided. I missed Takami but not in any sensual way. We had been lovers as well as friends but it was her smile and her sense of fun that I missed the most. But I was happy that she had found the answers to the questions that had haunted her, and that she now had a purpose for her life and a companion to share it. I had seen the way that she and Sheka had looked at each other. There would be no problems there.

And there were no problems between Kamose and me either. It was just like it had been at the beginning. He didn't even hide his feelings for me when we were at formal gatherings, he held my hand even when addressing his generals. And I think they loved him the more for it. I certainly did. It made me feel proud to be his queen. And the problems that had tormented him seemed to have disappeared as well. He seemed more relaxed, more confident. The trials he had undergone, which I could only imagine, seemed to have made him stronger. He was no longer an inexperienced young man, a king in name only. He was a man who commanded the respect as well as the love of his people. We took time to stop off at temples and even at some small villages along the river. We were welcomed wherever we landed, the crowds looking in awe at their king, a figure many of them had never seen before, and he spoke to the common people as well as to the priests.

Word had reached us that the capital was in safe hands, that Huya was in command of the army, and Teti was once again carrying out the duties of vizier, a task which no one could have done better. The man who had fouled the great office of vizier was in chains, awaiting the king's judgement. There were no enemies left to oppose the king or to trouble his people. We would soon be home, surrounded by family, and I felt a satisfaction that we had all done our duty and that the gods would surely find us worthy. And, if they did, then I had plans to make sure that not a single night would pass when Kamose and I would not try, several times if possible, to ensure the succession!

Kamose

To be home, at last, after so many trials. Everything seemed so much sweeter when we crossed our own borders. The river had never seemed so beautiful. The desert has a wonder of its own, its light and colour are unequalled anywhere else, but I had no wish to see quite so much of it again for a while. We took our time, especially when I heard from Huya that all was under control in the capital. And dear sweet Teti, still not able to retire! I could think of no further ways to reward his loyalty, he already had every award in my power, but I felt that my undying love and gratitude just might be the highest award he would value. The one that seemed most anxious to make progress was Amasis, and I sympathised with how much he must be missing his own family.

When we finally came in sight of the capital, with flags flying from the temples and from the palace walls, with trumpets sounding across the distance between us, I finally felt that I was home. There was Teti and Nefret and Kashta, Huya and Yrsa and their young daughter, Amaja and young Senwasre, and more well-wishers than there was space on the dockside to hold safely. When we were secured to the quayside, I left the ship holding my beloved Reja by the hand. I wanted people to see that I was not some remote, god-like figure they could not even look at directly. I was happy for them to think of me as a god after my time had finished but, for the moment, I was a man with a beautiful wife and a wonderful family. I offered them a royal vision of what so many of them had and valued for themselves. Family is everything. I embraced Teti and everyone else. The people cheered and then, finally, we all went home. I was utterly exhausted. There would be a great banquet later, with offerings at the temples and food available to everyone who came for it. But, for the moment, I just wanted time with family.

It was the following day when I had the man who I had trusted as my vizier brought before me. He was a pathetic sight. He knew his life was forfeit, that much went without saying. But he could save his soul for the afterlife by telling me what I wanted to know. Otherwise he would have no place in the company of the gods. He told me he had been approached by agents of Tarka, with promises of unlimited wealth and power, but he had seen through them. He had no interest in Tarka or his gold but felt he could use him to remove the one obstacle in the way of his own ambitions, me. He did not need to rule as Tarka's vassal. If I was removed he could just take the throne for himself and rule as my successor. Then he would have all of the wealth and power that even his vanity could crave. If that meant removing the queen and the rest of my family as well, that did not seem to bother him.

I was puzzled by the great diggings in the desert and at this he almost smiled. Tarka had believed the legends of the bottomless mines, where no man could ever go deep enough to reach the end, and had come up with the idea of digging a huge trench between the mines and the great river and causing the waters to be diverted away from our lands and into the deepest parts of the earth, down into the underworld itself, back to where many believed the waters originally came from. Ramose admitted he had almost laughed out loud when he heard this ridiculous idea, how could anyone hope to control a river so mighty, but it had given him an idea. By encouraging this madness he had kept Tarka busy and had occupied many of his resources, diverting them away from the north and giving him more room to make his own plans. He even had an idea of trying to convince Tarka to be present when the workings were opened in the hope he might be swallowed up by the waters. I followed his tale with genuine surprise, that he had so little regard for the enormous suffering of so many just to provide a distraction. This was not a man worthy of the slightest respect. And certainly not of a place among the gods. My judgement was that he be hanged, a most degrading death, and then his body burned. Nothing was to be left for the judgement before the gods. He was taken away sobbing and I felt nothing but relief that his plans had not been successful. It was obvious he would have shown no mercy to myself or anyone close to me.

I had other meetings during the day, with Teti and his staff to discuss the many aspects of the management of the kingdom that had been neglected in my absence, with Amasis to discuss the repair of the ships that had been worked so hard on the river, with Nehsi and Huya about the borders after so many months without the usual patrols and reports, and with any of my people who needed to speak of some genuine grievance. But for the moment I had to speak with Reja. She had been feeling a little unwell for the past few days. Some feelings of sickness, especially when she smelled or tasted food. Even dishes she normally enjoyed. We were not concerned that she was ill, that was not the reason I had summoned the physician, but her belly was looking distinctly rounded and her breasts were swelling, the tips darkening. We knew the signs. If the gods had finally answered our prayers and decided that I was, after all, worthy to take my place on the throne of the two lands, perhaps, this time, they would enable us to share the joy they had previously snatched from us, and make us the two happiest people in the kingdom. Then, surely, we could invite all of the family for a visit, and I would show off my son to my own father. And I could rest easy that there would be another Lord of the Two lands when my time came to join the gods.

END

Ian Lancaster is a retired academic with a passion for Ancient Egypt. He now writes novels and extended short stories, many with an Ancient Egyptian theme.

By the same author:

Conspiracy in the Sands (Egypt book 1)

A short story set in Ancient Egypt about a young man who loses a love and finds a mystery

Treason on the Nile (Egypt book 2)

In Ancient Egypt a young man is tasked by the king with restoring a desecrated tomb. Neither of them would have believed the danger that would follow for them both – and even for the kingdom itself.

Valley of Secrets (Egypt book 3)

The king of Egypt has been murdered and his family is in great danger. But who is the enemy?

Sceptre of the Gods (Egypt book 4)

A royal tomb has been violated and a foreign power threatens the king. How are these connected and what can he do to save his kingdom?

Labyrinth of Fear (Egypt book 5)

Part one.

A royal visit to a distant land brings new family ties and new experiences. Caught up in a cataclysm that changed the world, four young people face a battle for survival and an unexpected future.

Part two

A return home shows that the world has changed and the old order replaced. New trials and new perils must be faced but in a familiar landscape.

An Alliance of Kings (Egypt book 6)

Set mainly on and around the island of Crete, where three kings meet to form an alliance against a mysterious enemy, known as *The Sea People*. Old passions are reignited and new relationships are formed, but an unpredictable encounter leads to a tragic outcome.

The Curse of the Sea People (Egypt book 7)

The Sea People have returned and the island of Crete is in danger. A new king relies on family, where everyone has a role to play and each faces difficult challenges and adventures of their own.

These stories form a continuous narrative and follow the same principal characters, told in the first person, through interconnected adventures. There are some adult themes.

Destiny and Harmony

A tale of frustrated love and revenge, with a modern twist, set on the coast of Cornwall.

Amenophis and the Sun King

A young archaeology student inherits information about an undiscovered tomb in Egypt, a discovery potentially even greater than the tomb of Tutankhamun. There is just one condition – she must keep it a secret.

Essence of Evil

With his mind broken by experiences in the American Civil War, a young doctor returns home to Victorian England where his passion for the antiquities of ancient Egypt is matched only by his obsession for a beautiful girl he sees in a photograph. As he ruthlessly pursues her these two worlds collide with a terrifying conclusion.

Dreaming of Angels

An estranged couple rediscover their love for each other during a desperate cliff rescue on a remote Scottish island.

The Slave Girl and the Watcher

Set in Ancient Egypt, where a young slave girl unwillingly becomes involved in a plot to kill the king. She has only one ally, the formidable warrior who guards the king as he sleeps, the Night Watcher.

Mystery at Cliff Cottage

A brother and sister are reunited after their father's death. An enigmatic message leads to a mystery that threatens to spiral out of control. A modern story set on the coast of Cornwall.

The Long Night of the Bear

and other stories

A short novel

Accidently cast adrift in a storm, a lifeboat ends up on the shores of a remote island high in the Arctic. For the two survivors, the elements are not the only dangers they face.

The Exhibit

A short story

The story of a restless spirit, a young princess taken from her tomb in the Valley of the Kings by archaeologists and finding herself in a glass case in the British Museum of Victorian London. No longer able to find her way to the afterlife with the gods of her time, can her spirit ever find peace?

The Curator

A short story

Desperate times call for desperate measures, and for the curator of Ancient Egyptian relics in a small rural museum they are desperate times indeed. He can save his job by inheriting a magnificent collection of antiquities from a city businessman. There is only one small problem. He will have to kill him first.

The Collection

A short story

A visit to a remote country estate to help catalogue a collection of antiquities gives a young man the opportunity to meet a beautiful young woman, the grand daughter of the wealthy donor. An attempted robbery gives them the opportunity to become close and he dares to hope that she may share the feelings he has developed for her. A tale of frustrated love set in Victorian England.

The Raising of Kathryn Mitchell

A short story

In Victorian London a young trainee doctor struggles to find a corpse to learn the anatomy he needs to enable him to qualify. Unfortunately, after deciding to rob a grave, things do not go quite as planned when he finds himself the owner of a fresh body.

Seven Days in Winter (Part 1)

A mysterious suicide on a remote Scottish mountain leads a young Police Officer on a search for a psychopathic killer, a man obsessed with revenge against those who had looted an ancient Egyptian tomb guarded by his ancestors since the time of the pharaohs. To add complications, the officer falls in love with the victim's daughter, the killer's final target. The tale of a modern curse from an ancient time.

The Island of Lost Souls (Part 2)

This sequel to *Seven Days in Winter* sees Bob and Isobel taking a long-delayed honeymoon and becoming accidental witnesses to a mysterious case of drug smuggling. What then seems like a simple undercover investigation soon spirals out of control, plunging them both into a terrifying world where violence is common and life is cheap. This story contains many adult themes.

A Road Well Travelled (Part 3)

This sequel to *Island of Lost Souls* sees the nightmare which Bob and Isobel had thought they left behind return with a vengeance. The kidnap of their baby daughter tests their courage and their resourcefulness to the full, and a new friend tests their loyalty to each other. A happy outcome does not always mean a happy end-ing. Contains adult themes.

The Ties That Bind Us (Part 4)

This sequel to *A Road Well Travelled* is the fourth part of the story of Bob and Isobel Cameron. Promotion for Bob brings increasing loneliness for Isobel, and her involvement in an unfolding investigation throws their relationship into sharp focus. A new love appears and it is far from clear which of them will be happy. Contains adult themes.